EGGS UNSCRAMBLED

THE SHOOTING STAR SERIES

SIMON NORTHOUSE

Simon Northouse is contactable via:

simon@simonnorthouse.com or visit the author's website at https://www.subscribepage.com/author_simon_northouse_home or Facebook page https://www.facebook.com/simonnorthouse

Disclaimer: This is a work of satirical fiction. Names, characters, businesses, places, events, locales, and incidents are the products of the author's imagination or used in a fictitious manner. Any resemblance to actual persons, living or dead, or actual events, is purely coincidental.

Published by Flabbergasted Publishing

First Edition

Kindle e-book ISBN-13:9780648968405

Paperback ISBN-13:9780648968412

Hardback ISBN-13:978-0-6489684-5-0

CONTENTS

1: The Proposition

I feel quite giddy and lightheaded at my wife's unexpected suggestion.

'Camping!' I exclaim. The very proposition fills me with dread. 'At Easter? Over my dead body!'

'Don't sound so alarmed. I haven't asked you to be neutered,' Fiona says as she hands me one end of a bedsheet, which we begin to fold.

'Why would you want to go camping? We live in a six-bedroom converted barn with two en-suites, four bathrooms, a massive dining and living room, a state-of-the-art kitchen and we have rural views to die for with a river at the end of our garden. And you want to rough it. I've never understood the appeal.'

'It will be fun, exciting. You know… action and adventure.'

'If you want action and adventure, we can stream the latest James Bond film on our 65" plasma TV while relaxing in our massage chairs. I went camping when I was a kid. It was hellish. The moment we arrived the heavens opened up. It didn't stop raining until we pulled into the driveway back home. There were daddy long legs in the tomato soup. Slugs invaded the bread. The sleeping bags got soaked. There was mud everywhere and our only form of entertainment was listening to the shipping forecast on the bloody radio.'

'You had an unpleasant experience, that's all. Anyway, it will be good for Mary… and the other kids.' I pass her the corners of the sheet and she begins to fold it into quarters.

'What other kids?' I ask, as a glug of adrenalin pumps into my bloodstream.

'Wallace, Robert, Sally, and Katrina,' she replies as I'm handed one end of a duvet cover.

'Why would camping be good for Wallace, Robert, Sally, and Katrina?' She gives me her stare specifically reserved for halfwits. I'm becoming extremely nervous about the direction this conversation is heading.

'We could all go together, like one big happy family.' I know what's coming next, but I'm clinging onto a slender thread I may have jumped the gun and misinterpreted her true intentions.

'Do you mean, we take the other kids along as playmates for Mary?'

She frowns at me. 'You can be really dense sometimes. No, I mean we all go, *all* four families.' I drop the corners of the duvet cover and sit down on the edge of the bed. 'I've been chatting with the girls.' It gets worse. 'They all think it's a wonderful idea. We've been doing some research online.' I'm hyperventilating. 'We don't have to rough it. We can hire a luxury motorhome for about £150 a day. They have a double bed, bunks, kitchen, toilet, and shower, plus plenty of storage. There's an awning that pulls out so we can have our own little outside area. They come fully equipped with everything we need. All we'd have to buy are three camping chairs and a portable table.' It appears Fiona's idea has already been rubber-stamped. A thought springs to mind, a thought that could save us all, well… me specifically, from this calamitous farce. Time for a bit of my finest acting.

'That all sounds well and good, Fiona, but I see at least two minor problems that will stop this particular hot-air balloon from rising.'

'Oh, and what's that?'

'Two numbskulls known as Robbo and Geordie.' I know for a fact Robbo is allergic to any form of outside activity and Geordie has an irrational hatred for people who own caravans… or motorhomes for that matter. This little duck is dead in the water.

'You don't think they'd be keen on the idea?' she replies as I pick up the duvet again and begin to fold.

'Keen! They'd rather feed their John Thomas into a meat grinder.' Disaster has been averted. My breathing has resumed, my blood pressure is falling, and the palpitations have almost ceased. She looks crestfallen and I feel a pang of guilt. I said a pang… not enough for me to reconsider.

'That's a shame. But *if* we could persuade Robbo and Geordie to go camping, would you be willing to give it a try?' I hand the duvet cover back to her and place my hands on her shoulders, safe in the knowledge the dum-dum twins will scoff at the suggestion.

'Of course, sweetheart. Now I think of it, it's actually not a bad idea. A motorhome would be far less hassle than a tent. I'd really enjoy it, us all being together, a large, harmonious extended family,' I lie as I peck her on the forehead. 'But alas, some things are not meant to be. You're right, it is a shame, but I can guarantee you that Robbo and Geordie will not even consider the proposition.' With my domestic chores complete, and the outlandish camping caper nipped in the bud, I turn to head out of the door.

'Oh, Will?'

'Yes, Fiona.'

'I was speaking with Julie and Jackie this morning.' I freeze. I sense a pre-emptive tactical strike. Is that an air-raid siren and the ominous rumble of heavy diesel engines I can hear?

'About?'

'The camping idea.' A battalion of Panzer tanks sweeps by my western flank, crushing all in their wake.

'Oh,' is all I can muster as my fight or flight response renders me immobile.

'And they said that Robbo and Geordie think it's a wonderful idea. And of course, Flaky and Gillian are already keen campers.' Another division of Panzers zooms by my eastern flank. 'We've all agreed we'll set off on the Saturday before Easter Sunday.' Stuka's overhead. 'Geordie has already narrowed it down to two possible camping grounds for us to stop at. Somewhere nice, near the beach, for a week. I'm glad you're willing to give it a go.' Blitzkrieg is complete. Outflanked, outgunned, out of my depth, and caught off-guard, I head downstairs and lay on the couch with a cushion over my head and feel sorry for myself. *No, please God, why me? I'm not a bad man.*

2: The Arrival

Our convoy of motorhomes snakes their way through the little seaside resort of Flexley-on-Sea.

'What a pretty little town,' Fiona gasps. 'It has everything we'll need. I've spotted a small supermarket, café's, restaurants, a fish and chip shop, and a curry house.'

'And at least three pubs. Old-fashioned ones as well. They're the best.' Fiona throws me a disapproving glance.

'Will, remember this is a family holiday. I don't want you disappearing with Robbo and Geordie for hours on end to the local pubs. You're here to spend quality time with your family.'

I offer her my most loving smile. 'And that's exactly what I intend to do, my little cherub. But it is my holiday too and I don't see any harm in having a couple of quiet pints each day. We'll find a friendly pub with a beer garden and we can take the children along.' She eyeballs me suspiciously for a moment before her expression melts into a smile.

'Well... it is nice to sit in a beer garden when the weather is as glorious as this.'

'That's the spirit.' I gaze out at the rippling water of the Bristol Channel on my right.

'The sea doesn't look very enticing,' she murmurs. 'It's brown.'

'It's an estuary. That's the silt that gets kicked up with the tides. It's perfectly fine to swim in.' She doesn't appear convinced. 'Somerset is a really beautiful county. Did you come here much when you were growing up?'

'Not that I can remember. You forget I grew up at the seaside. For holidays we'd usually visit London or head north and into the hills.'

'Daddy, are we nearly there, yet?' Mary asks for the umpteenth time. I peer at her through the rearview mirror and take a quick glance at the sat-nav.

'Yes, we are, sweetpea. Another ten minutes and we'll be at the campsite.'

'Daddy?'

'Yes, Mary.'

'Is there a beach at our campsite?'

'Yes, Mary. According to Uncle Geordie, there's a beach.'

'Daddy, are we sleeping in this caravan tonight?'

'Yes, we are. And it's called a motorhome, not a caravan. You've asked me these questions a hundred times, already. There's a beach, a funfair in the town, and an animal farm for us to visit on an actual farm.'

'Aw, she's excited, that's all,' Fiona whispers. As we leave Flexley behind, the coastal road rises. Inland, undulating fields of lush grass are dotted with sheep and their newborn lambs.

'I don't see why Geordie couldn't have driven down with the rest of us. He's always got to rush off ahead,' I grumble, peering at my wing mirrors to confirm Robbo and Flaky are still behind us.

'I think he wanted to get there early so he could erect the tent.'

'He's always got to be different, hasn't he? Why couldn't he hire a campervan and make life easy.'

'It's not your problem.'

'Believe me, Geordie is a problem, he's everyone's problem. He likes to share.'

'In 500 metres, your destination will be on the right,' announces the posh lady from inside the sat-nav. I stare out at the landscape that stretches towards the sea before it abruptly stops.

'Hmm…' I inadvertently mumble.

'What?' Fiona quizzes.

'Nothing.' The terrain doesn't fill me full of good cheer but I'm not going to articulate my fears… not yet anyway.

'You have arrived at your destination,' Mrs posh sat-nav announces. A waist-high stone wall demarcates the boundary to a field. I turn right and navigate past an open farm gate, hitting a massive pothole as I do so.

'Christ! The bloody farmer needs to get that filled in. It's like a bomb crater.' I survey the campsite. It's rectangular and probably a good 4 hectares in size as it slopes away towards the sea. The close-cropped grass is peppered with sheep droppings.

'Oh, my! This is majestic!' Fiona exclaims.

'Are we here?' Mary screeches.

'Yep. We're here.' In the middle of the field are Geordie's Range Rover and trailer. He's removing various things from the roof rack. Wallace and Robert are running around playing a game of tag as Jackie pulls items from the boot of the car. 'Looks like they've only just arrived.'

'The views are stunning, and there's no one else here. We've got it all to ourselves. Not another camper in sight,' Fiona says, excitedly. We slowly edge down the gentle incline. As we near the Kincaid family, I notice a row of about 8 standpipes and power outlets sticking out of the ground.

'Ah, good. We have power and water,' I comment.

'We have our own power and water. That's why we hired a motorhome,' Fiona replies.

'Yes, but it's always good to have a backup.' I park the van opposite Geordie, as Fiona and Mary hurriedly unclip their seatbelts and leap from the vehicle. I climb out as Flaky and Robbo park up their vans alongside. Within seconds there are five excitable kids running around. Geordie appears unusually enthused with proceedings as he continues to unload bags of camping gear.

'Ah! The glampers arrive!' he shouts, grinning at me. Jackie appears less enthused. Fiona, Julie, and Gillian circle her, offering help.

'Can you believe he booked a campsite that doesn't have an ablutions block? What was he thinking?' I do a quick 360 around the field. It's true. There is no shower or toilet block. In fact, the field is barren of any structure.

'Calm down, woman. I have a portable shower tent we can hook up to the water mains and the farmer said he'd be along today to dig a latrine for us.' Jackie crosses her arms and throws her husband a fierce glare.

'If you think I'm taking cold showers every day and squatting over a hole in the ground, open for everyone to see, you've got another think coming!' she shouts.

'I have a privacy screen. What do you take me for?' he replies.

'Jackie, don't worry,' Gillian says, 'you can use the shower and toilet in our motorhome.'

'Yes, of course you can,' adds Fiona. 'We've all agreed that everyone can use each other's amenities in the vans. It will be like a commune,' she giggles. Jackie unfolds her arms and smiles graciously at her friends as she gives them a group hug.

'Thank you, girls,' she says. I turn and jump back into the cab.

'Where are you going?' Robbo asks.

'Reconnaissance. Hop in.' Flaky, who has been unusually quiet so far, looks up at me with a concerned expression.

'I think I'll join you,' he says, tentatively.

'Be back in a minute,' I shout to Fiona as I start the engine. We trundle off down the hill, heading towards the sea. 'I have an uneasy feeling about this.'

'Me too,' Robbo agrees.

'It doesn't look promising. Let's hope we're wrong,' Flaky adds. I park up at the end of the campground. We sit in silence and stare out at the scene. A three-wire farm fence establishes the boundary between private and public property. About three metres beyond the fence is a well-worn coastal path. Beyond that is another few metres of verdant, spongy grass—then—the horizon. We jump out of the vehicle, slip easily through the wire fence, and walk on. All three of us tiptoe reluctantly to the edge and peer over.

'Jesus H Christ and pockets of blood,' Robbo mumbles as he pulls a spliff out and sparks up.

'Oh dear, what was the moron thinking. A campsite on the edge of a cliff,' Flaky murmurs, shaking his head.

'That's a hundred-foot drop!' I whisper as I stare at the craggy cliff face and the rocks far below which are being pounded by seething waves. There's a good mile or so of clifftop before it drops away to meet flat sandy beaches to the north and south. A few miles to the right is Flexley-on-Sea. To the left, more beach, broken only by what appears to be a river. 'Come on, let's get back,' I say. As we drive up the paddock towards the others Flaky begins his first lecture.

'I can't believe you let Geordie pick the campsite. What were you thinking? This is typical! We have five children under the age of eight and that idiot picks a site that is on the edge of a cliff.'

'I didn't *let* Geordie pick it. He took it upon himself. Anyway, we're camping at the top of the field so we're not that close to the cliff.'

'Oh, that's all right then. Because we all know that children don't wander!' Flaky snipes.

'Flaky, I'm not disagreeing with you. We'll give the kids a stern warning about not going past the boundary fence. But you're right, it's not ideal.'

'There's only one thing for it. We need to find a more suitable site.'

'You'll be lucky,' Robbo drawls. 'We must have passed at least ten sites along the way and every one of them had "no vacancy" signs.'

'Robbo's right, Flaky. It's the Easter weekend, the weather has been great, and it's forecast to continue. The hottest April for years. You know what the British are like once the Sun comes out— they head to the coast in their droves. Let's suck it and see. It's been a long drive, it's nearly 3 pm and I for one don't intend to traipse around looking for a new campsite. We'll talk about it tomorrow. Let's not start the holiday on a sour note with our misgivings about the bloody cliff. Look on the bright side, we have the whole place to ourselves... at the moment.'

'I suppose you're right,' Flaky says as he calms down. 'Don't you find it odd though?'

'What?'

'That there are no other campers. Especially as everywhere else is chock-full.'

I contemplate for a moment. 'Yeah... it is odd.'

'There're no amenities, that's why,' Robbo explains. 'Who wants to camp in a field with no toilets or showers? It's not the 1970s. People expect a certain level of sophistication these days.'

I let out a long sigh. 'I hope that's the reason and not something more untoward.'

3: The Erection

We take less than twenty minutes to arrange the camper vans in a slight arc, pull out tables and chairs, erect a portable barbeque and unfurl the awnings. Meanwhile, Geordie is still unpacking camping gear from the trailer. I saunter over to him.

'Geordie, it's a delightful spot but I'm worried about the cliffs,' I say as Robbo and Flaky join us.

'In what way?' he asks appearing baffled.

'There are four six-year-olds and one seven-year-old,' Flaky begins. 'Large drops and children don't mix.'

'Don't worry about the bairns,' Geordie sniffs, 'they'll be fine. I'll have a word with them.'

'I think we're asking for trouble camping here,' Flaky continues. 'And I'm not alone. Will and Robbo are of the same mindset.'

Geordie snorts. 'What's wrong with you lot. You cannae wrap your children up in cotton wool all their lives. They need to be free to roam and explore. They need to learn from their mistakes. That's what gives them tenacity and resilience in life. If you had your way, you'd still be spoon-feeding them porridge when they're thirty and tucking them in for the night. They need to be weaned off the titty at some point.'

12

'They're not going to learn from their mistakes if they fall off the bloody cliff, are they?' Flaky shouts. Geordie gazes at each of us.

'I tell you what, I'll have a quiet word with them now if it makes you feel any better,' he says in a conciliatory manner. 'Wallace, Robert! Come over here. And bring the girls with you.' The children run over to him. 'Right, turn around. Can you see the sea in the distance?'

'Yes,' they all murmur, slightly bemused.

'Now, can you see where the land stops?' They all nod their heads. 'That's a cliff, an extremely dangerous cliff. You fall off it and you're dead, then you'll be in big trouble. *Keep away from it.* Do I make myself clear?'

'Give me strength,' Flaky whispers. Mary and Katrina appear visibly upset at the news of their impending death.

'But I don't want to die,' Katrina sobs.

'No, nor me,' Mary says as her bottom lip quivers uncontrollably. 'We haven't even started our holiday, yet.'

'You're not going to die,' I offer gently as I kneel and put my arms around them.

'But Uncle Geordie said we were going to fall off the cliff and if we do, we'll be in trouble and dead,' Mary sniffs.

'I didnae say that,' Geordie says, mystified by the girl's interpretation of his dire warning.

'What Uncle Geordie meant to say was, the cliffs are a dangerous place. If you keep away from them, you can't fall off them, can you?'

'The rule is that no one is allowed outside of the wire fence,' Flaky adds. The girls stop crying as I wipe their tears away with the pad of my thumb.

'What if there's an earthquake?' Wallace says with feverish excitement. 'Will we all fall off the cliff and die, then?' He appears genuinely thrilled at the prospect.

'There won't be an earthquake,' Geordie replies.

'You don't know that. What about a hurricane, or a tornado, or tidal wave?'

'Wallace, there'll be none of those things,' Geordie says, becoming impatient.

'What about a volcano? Or what if an asteroid smashes into us and the whole world splits in two and all the Zombies rise up from the dead and try to eat us?'

'Right! Enough! Run along, I can hear your mother calling you,' Geordie snaps. The children all turn tail and run towards the campervans.

'That went well,' Flaky says. 'You certainly have a way with words when it comes to children.' Geordie resumes his unpacking.

'Aye, well, no good sugar-coating it. A wee fright will do them good,' he says as he throws another bag onto the grass.

'Bloody hell, Geordie! How much gear have you brought?' Robbo asks.

'Just the bare necessities to make life enjoyable.'

'The bare necessities!' Robbo says with incredulity. 'You've got enough crap here to billet a small army.' Geordie gives him the evil eye.

'Hey, unlike you three milksops, I'm doing it the real way, the hard way, nature's way. I've always had an affinity with the great outdoors. It's part of my Gaelic heritage. It makes me feel alive. Man versus wild. Living off your wits, a battle against the elements, tested to the very core of your psyche. Life or death.'

'You're camping on the Somerset coast. It's not like you're pitching a tent on the north side of the Eiger during a blizzard,' I remind him. 'Anyway, give me my home comforts any day of the week. Shower, toilet, fridge, heating and cooling, a comfy bed, and protection from the elements.'

Geordie sneers at me. 'You English have always been soft. Anyway, how much do those bloody things cost to hire for a week?' he says, nodding at the motorhomes.

'Just shy of £1500,' Flaky responds.

'A fool and their money,' he sneers. 'This lot cost me eight hundred quid and it will last a lifetime,' he adds with an element of pride, as he nods at the camping paraphernalia.

'It'll take you a lifetime to put the bloody lot together,' Robbo chuckles. 'The size of that tent is ridiculous, and why have you got two?'

'The big one is for me and Jackie, and the small dome tent is for the boys.'

'Why have you got a separate one for the boys?'

Geordie offers a wry smile. 'Why do you think, sunshine?' he says in a whisper as he glances over at the women who are busy preparing snacks for the children.

'Ah, I see,' Robbo says. 'You're not as gormless as you look.'

15

'That's right. I hope you three enjoy your seven days of celibacy. But I won't be missing out on my nuptials just because we're bloody camping.'

'I'm going to grab a cup of tea then freshen up with a shower,' I say as I turn to leave.

'I think I'll join you,' Robbo says.

'They're quite narrow shower units, Robbo. Not sure they'll accommodate two of us, but we can give it a whirl,' I say.

'Ha ha, most amusing.'

'You three aren't going anywhere. You can help me put this bloody lot together,' Geordie says, nodding at the mass of equipment laid out on the grass which now resembles a car boot sale on a busy public holiday.

'I thought it was man versus wild. A battle of wits against the elements. One man, alone, tested to the very core of his psyche. Surely you don't need the help of three English milksops?' I reply.

'I'm more than capable of putting this camp together single-handedly, but I thought it would be a salutary lesson for you three in the art of bushcraft. In a few months' time, we'll be stranded on a desert island, making a TV show. This is good practice. Watch, listen, and inwardly digest.'

'Abandoned on an island in the South Pacific during cyclone season is not comparable to camping in England during an unseasonably warm spring.' Flaky adds.

Geordie glares at him. 'It's about the art of improvisation, motivation, and tenacity. Now, are you lot going to help me or are you away to your luxury motorhomes?'

'Personally, I'd pick my motorhome,' Robbo says pulling a joint out of his shirt pocket.

'Come on,' I say, resigned to the inevitable. 'Let's give the knucklehead a hand, then when it's done, we can start enjoying ourselves.' Geordie unzips the tent bags, carefully extracts all the contents, and lays them out on the ground.

'Christ, there's a lot of gear!' Robbo notes. Indeed, there is. Poles, ropes, canvas, bags of nuts, bolts, rubber widgets and odd-looking fasteners.

'Are you sure this is a tent? It looks more like the parts to the space shuttle. Why didn't you buy a simple dome tent like you've got for the boys?' I inquire.

'They're no good for a man of my size. I need room to stand up and breathe.' He hands Robbo the manual. 'Robbo, you can read the instructions out.'

'Why me?'

'Because I've seen you in action before putting things together. You're bloody hopeless. You can barely make your own bed. At least you can make yourself useful reading the instructions.'

'You don't need instructions to erect a tent,' I scoff. 'Look at the picture on the front of the bag and figure it out from there. You're not building a scale model of the Taj Mahal!'

Geordie stares at me and shakes his head. 'That's the problem with you, Bill. You go tearing off ahead, ignoring convention and protocol. Don't you remember Haslops Fables? The rabbit and the hare?'

'It's Aesop's Fables, and it's the tortoise and the hare, you moron,' Flaky corrects.

17

'Whatever!' Geordie yells. 'The point is still the same. Billy Boy is the hare, always going off half-cocked, winging it, playing it by ear. An unrestrained zephyr blowing hither and thither on the barren sand dunes of the Serengeti. A rudderless raft bobbing about in the ocean of life. No structure. Someone has gone to a lot of trouble to put those instructions together and we're going to follow them... to the letter! You all know my motto in life—get it right first time, on time, every time. Saves a lot of heartache down the track.'

'I've never heard you say that motto before,' Flaky queries.

'Come on, let's get on with it,' I say, already frustrated with the situation.

Robbo clears his throat as he studies the manual. 'Ahem, take pole 1 and join with pole B.' Geordie rolls the poles around until he spots what he wants.

'Here we go, pole 1 and pole B,' he states in a cheery tone as he passes me the poles. I push them into one another.

'Now, take pole 2 and join with pole C,' Robbo continues. Geordie hands another two poles to Flaky who joins them together.

'Now take the cross-grunt-bearer and slip it into the flubber corset,' Robbo says.

'Take what and slip it into what corset?' Geordie says scratching his head.

'The cross-grunt-bearer and slip it into the flubber corset,' Robbo repeats, as he studies the parts list. 'Ah, the grunt bearer is that long pole there and the flubber corset is that hollow rubber bung next to it.'

'Of course, I see,' Geordie replies, as he pushes the grunt-bearer through the flubber corset.'

18

'Align the hole on each end of the bearer with the spangle-sprocket of pole 1 and pole B.'

'What the hell's a spangle sprocket?' Geordies asks as he rubs at his chin.

I'm losing patience fast. 'It's perfectly obvious. There's a hole at both ends of the bearer. There's a spike on top of both poles. Place the bloody spikes through the holes,' I snap.

He glares back at me. 'You know, a wise man once said, "impatience is an unsuitable bedfellow for excellence". You should pay heed to those words, old pal.'

'Whoever this "so-called" wise man was, he'd evidently never helped you erect a tent.' After another laborious ten minutes, we have constructed a simple rectangle that our children could have put together in about two minutes.

'Okay, now for the canopy,' Robbo says. Geordie unfolds the enormous khaki coloured canvas tent. 'Take corner X and corner N and place over the quadrangulated bi-angle. Then take corner Z and corner 1 and place over the vertiginous adjacent opposing quadrangulated bi-angle.' I'm tiring of this charade.

'Where exactly did you buy this tent?' I inquire.

'I got it online,' Geordie replies.

'You get a lot of things online, these days,' I say. Geordie and Flaky each grab one corner of the tent.

'Unlike you, Bill, I'm a 21st century man. You can get a bargain online. The days of bricks and mortar shops belong to a bygone era.'

'Have you forgotten he's the renaissance man?' Robbo says, grinning at me.

'Almost,' I say. With much effort and swearing, we manoeuvre the heavy canvas over the first part of the frame. 'No, no, no! This is all wrong,' I declare. 'There's no pitch.'

Geordie turns to me. 'What do you mean?'

'A tent needs a pitch to allow water to run off, otherwise, it will pool in the middle.'

'What do the instructions say?' Geordie says, squinting at Robbo as the Sun blazes into his eyes.

'Hang on a mo. Ah, here we go. Yes, there is an "A" frame that is erected inside the tent once we place the canvas over the outer-frame.'

'Ha! Care to eat your own words?' Geordie snorts at me.

'No. But I'd like to eat something. I'm bloody starving,' I reply as Jackie ambles over to us.

'Boys, how much longer do you think you'll be with the tent?'

'About four years,' Robbo says. Jackie ignores him.

'We've fed the children, but we thought it would be nice if all the adults sat down together for our first camping meal. It's only a snack, mind.'

'About another twenty minutes, dear, then we'll be done,' Geordie replies. His estimate is extremely optimistic in my humble opinion.

'Okay. Well, me and the girls are going to chill and have a glass of white wine… get into the holiday mode.'

'Lucky for some,' Robbo grumbles as she disappears.

My tolerance is nearing its expiration date. 'Look, let's take the canvas off, get the "A" frame erected then fit the canvas, as it's typically done. Call me a traditionalist. I don't care what the instructions say, we need the frame up first, then the tent,' I advise.

'Fine, we'll do it your way, Bill. Some may call it reckless to bypass an expertly written instruction manual, but on your head be it. Don't say I didn't warn you.'

'I won't.'

'Robbo, skip to the erection of the "A" frame,' Geordie orders.

'Right, where was I?' Robbo murmurs as he flicks through the pages. 'This manual's bigger than War and Peace. Ah, here we go. Attach the flangle-tube to the gear loft splice and thread through the spatchcock relucter release mechanism. Next, screw the wing dangle to the crotch exciter and place it over the transient cleat bob, making sure you don't over tension. Push the thrust giblet through the perturbed nipple adjuster and hold it in place with the stressed vibration fibulator. Tighten the cripple shank… one and a quarter widdershins in a numerical anticlockwise direction. Hang on… there's a warning. Do not over-tighten the cripple shank otherwise, damage to the flucker arm may occur.'

'Slow down!' Geordie yells. 'I cannae keep up. Take it one step at a time.'

'That is one step,' Robbo replies, peering at the booklet with a furrowed brow.

I turn to Flaky. 'I've had enough of this circus. Come on, we'll put the dome tent up for the boys.'

'Good idea. We're going deeper down the rabbit hole here,' he replies.

'Geordie, where do you want us to pitch the boys tent?' I ask.

'Not too far away, but not too close either.' Ask a silly question. We grab the tent and tip the contents out about fifteen feet away. I join the poles together as Flaky lays out the main tent. Robbo persists with the instruction manual.

'Take the second perturbed nipple adjuster and insert it firmly into the crotch exciter, making sure not to overstretch the rubber flange squelcher.' Robbo scratches at his head for a moment. 'Are you sure this manual is for a tent? It sounds more like a script for a porno movie!'

'Just read the bloody instructions!' Geordie shouts, becoming increasingly agitated.

Ten minutes later, Flaky and I have erected the dome tent.

'That was relatively easy,' Flaky says, smiling.

'If you two have finished fannying around over there, you can put up the shower tent,' Geordie commands. We both stare at the contraption of poles that Geordie is constructing.

'Hell's bells,' Flaky whispers. 'It looks like the framework to the Bilbao Guggenheim Museum.' We saunter back to the construction site. I pick up the tent bag and study the picture on the front. It has a label stitched to the side that intrigues me.

'Geordie, do you realise this tent was designed in Norway?'

'What of it? The Norwegians are well known for their innovation and technical expertise.'

'But it was manufactured in North Korea,' I add.

'Your point being?'

'Will's point is, it's illegal to buy anything from North Korea. Most of the world has blacklisted them,' Flaky states.

'Oh, I'm quaking in my boots,' Geordie sneers. 'I'm sure a CIA snatch squad have already been dispatched to extradite me to Guantanamo Bay.'

'Designed in Norway by scientists, manufactured in North Korea by technicians, assembled in England by a fuckwit,' Robbo chortles.

'Hey, less of the smart-arse comments and more clear explanations wouldn't go amiss,' Geordie barks.

'Okay, you asked for it,' Robbo says. 'Connect the griddle plumper to the quim jiggler and insert into the inverted fruckle hole.' Geordie's patience has finally been exhausted.

'Jesus Christ!' he explodes. 'Give me those bloody instructions! You're making this up!' He snatches the manual from Robbo and scans the pages. 'Who wrote this bloody crap! Clearly, some foreigner who can barely speak English!' he yells.

'Yep, possibly Scottish,' Robbo says, with obvious glee. 'I think something has got lost in translation. From Norwegian to Korean to English is a path fraught with many dangers.' Jackie re-emerges on the scene as Flaky and I swiftly tackle the shower tent.

'Geordie, I thought you said it would take you twenty minutes? You're no further on than when I left. What's wrong with you. Can you not erect a simple tent in a timely manner?' she quizzes.

'There's nothing simple about this bloody tent,' Geordie bellows. 'Foreign shite!'

'I told you not to buy it off the internet, you never know what you're going to get. Why didn't you go down to the local camping store as I suggested?'

'Thank you for your twenty-twenty hindsight, dear. Now, if you don't mind, we have work to do.'

'Suit yourself, but us girls aren't waiting any longer. We're going to eat,' she says as she marches off.

'She has no appreciation of the things I do for her,' he grumbles.

'It's warming up,' Robbo says. 'I'm going to change into my shorts and flip-flops.' I stare wearily at Robbo as he departs, then fix my attention to the half-built tent frame and the many poles and fittings still to assemble.

'For God's sake, Geordie, this tent is bloody huge!'

'I've told you, I'm a tall man. I need the space.'

'A tent is for sleeping in. You spend most of the time outside. That's what camping's about.'

'There! That's the shower done,' Flaky announces, quite proud of his achievement. I wander over to Geordie, pick up the ridiculous manual, and look at the sketches of the final erected tent.

'This is the oddest tent I've ever seen. It's like a McMansion!' I study the general arrangement layout for a moment. Flaky joins me and peers at the instructions over my shoulder.

'Ah! I see. There are three parts to it. This front bit here,' he says pointing at the sketch, 'this is the entrance but serves as the covered outdoor eating area. Then, a sort of vestibule, and behind that, the bedroom. We need to look at it as three unique structures with the "A" frame running down the middle, like a spine. I suggest we dismantle everything, assemble the "A" frame as a standalone, then fix it to the uprights. It's a bit like building a house.'

'Yeah, I think you're right. Let's start from scratch,' I say as Robbo returns clad in his holiday gear. We disassemble everything, throw the instruction manual away and work as a team using our common sense to rebuild the tent. After fifteen minutes, it's taking shape. But as with most construction projects, there're always unforeseen issues.

'No, Geordie! Forget about the frigging wing dangle and crotch exciter! It's obvious that cross piece attaches to the upright pole!' I shout.

'Shouldn't we have a perturbed nipple adjuster on that, though?' Robbo queries.

I point at a wing nut attached to the pole. 'That is the bloody nipple adjuster. It's used to heighten or lower the pole.' We soldier on for another forty minutes until the frame is complete. Another ten minutes slip by as we adjust, loosen, and re-tighten various nuts and attachments until everything is level and aligned. We stand back to admire our handiwork as a raucous cackle of laughter emanates from the other side of the motorhomes.

'How many bottles do you reckon they've gone through?' Robbo asks.

I scrunch up my face. 'From the volume of their laughter, I'd say they're well into their third. Where are the kids?'

'I checked on them a moment ago,' Flaky begins. 'They're in your van watching a Harry Potter film.'

'Great! This is what camping is all about; the kids watching a DVD inside, the women outside, noisily getting hammered on white wine, and four mugs sweating their gonads off trying to erect a canvas tower block manufactured by a blackballed country. Come on, let's get this bloody monstrosity finished. I'd like to start my holiday soon.' Flaky and I grab one side of the canvas, Robbo, and Geordie the other.

'Okay, lift,' Flaky orders. We slide the canvas along the frame until it's sat snugly in position. I glance down at the wall of the tent, smile, and nod to Flaky.

'Take a look at that,' I murmur as I pull a tissue out and wipe my brow. Flaky stares at the stencilled portrait on the canvas and grins.

'The great man himself. Geordie's never going to get this tent mistaken for someone else's.' I glance over at Geordie and Robbo, who are also looking at something which is causing them great puzzlement.

'What's the matter?' I ask, barely able to contain myself.

'There's massive bloody lettering etched onto the side,' Geordie replies. 'It must be the tent maker's logo.'

'What does it say?'

'Buggered if I know. Just the letters DPRK.'

'Take a look on this side,' Flaky says as I bite down on my tongue. Geordie and Robbo saunter around.

'Kiss my bright blue arse!' Geordie exclaims as Robbo cracks up laughing. 'Is that who I think it is?'

'Yep, it's the rocket man,' I snigger.

4: The Farmer

The laughter from the women grows louder.

'I'm glad someone's having a good time,' Flaky mumbles.

'Come on, lads, nearly there. We just need to peg it down, attach the guy ropes, fit the groundsheet, assemble the tables and chairs, set up the kitchen area, pull out the barbeque and we're done,' I say, trying to keep positive.

'What time does it get dark?' Robbo moans sarcastically. We spend the next fifteen minutes hammering in pegs. The tent has more guy ropes than a Big Top Circus. By the time we've nearly finished, we're all filthy, dripping with sweat and wounded. Robbo split his big toe open on a tent peg. Flaky copped a savage blow to the head when he stood up too quickly and collided with the lump hammer Geordie was holding above him. I picked up a painful splinter in my thumb and Geordie nearly garrotted himself on a guy rope.

'Nearly done,' Geordie says trying to force a smile. 'It didn't take too long, after all.' I check my watch, it's nearly 5 pm.

'No, only two hours, which is the equivalent of eight man-hours,' I moan.

'You've got a very negative side to you, Bill. You need to keep it in check otherwise it will consume you.'

'Thanks for the advice,' I reply sternly as the rumble of a diesel engine comes into earshot. We turn around and stare up the field towards the entrance. An old tractor with a front loader bucket is heading our way.

'Ah, here comes Farmer Clarence Longdon to dig the latrine,' Geordie declares with a smile.

'Farmer Long Dong?' Robbo sniggers.

Geordie eyes him wearily. 'Long… don,' he articulates. The tractor rattles down the hill spewing black plumes of diesel smoke into the pristine air. He pulls up alongside us and stops the engine.

'Which one of you be called, Geordie?' he asks, in a strong west country brogue. A floppy, moth-eaten hat rests on his head above a dirty white collarless shirt ensconced within a faded red waistcoat, its one button struggles gallantly to hold in his ample belly. His face is as wrinkled as a prune, his skin, a weather-beaten old shammy leather.

'I'm Geordie,' the big man replies. The farmer stands and beams at us. We're greeted with a row of rotten blackened and yellow teeth not dissimilar to a decrepit picket fence. A blue piece of twine is used as a belt to hold up his grimy trousers. He sports Wellington boots, one black, the other, green.

'I'm Clarence Longdon and I take it you're my campers?' he states eyeing the motorhomes suspiciously.

'Actually, no, we're the British Bobsleigh Team training for the next Winter Olympics,' I joke. His left eye scrunches up as he lets out a little groan.

'Oh, a joker, eh?'

'Ignore that idiot, Clarence. Pleased to meet you,' Geordie says shaking his hand as he introduces the rest of us. Clarence pulls a stub of a rollie out from behind his ear, sticks it in his mouth and lights up. He stares at Geordie's tent.

'I ain't seen a tent that big since they stationed the US Marines here before D-Day. It's an odd bugger,' he murmurs to no one in particular.

'Have you come to dig the latrine?' Geordie asks.

'That be right… and collect my money. We said cash, didn't we?' I can tell by Geordie's surprised expression the idiot hasn't any cash on him.

'£20 a day, wasn't it?'

'Aye. Plus, another £30 for digging the latrine and £5 per day for water and electricity.'

'We won't be using the water or electricity,' Flaky informs him.

'Don't matter none if you use it or not. Not my concern. It's still £5 per day.' Geordie does some quick calculations.

'Okay, £25 per day, times by four equals one hundred, times by seven, equals seven hundred.'

'And the latrine,' the farmer adds.

'Oh, yes. So that brings it to a grand total of £730. Robbo, get your wallet out.'

'Eh up! Why have I got to get my wallet out?' he says, looking wounded.

'Because you're always cashed up and I don't have any money on me.' It is true, Robbo always carries a large roll of notes on him. He sighs as he retrieves his bulging wallet, counts out the notes and slaps them into the outstretched hand of Clarence. He sniffs the money and chuckles before rolling them up and sticking the wad down the front of his pants.

'Is it long dong by name and long dong by nature?' Robbo sniggers. Clarence smirks back as he grabs at the inside of his upper thigh.

'Both. Bit of a lady's man, I am. I have a different woman every night,' he declares. The lying get! 'I'm on three dating apps. Women can't get enough of me.' I doubt that very much.

'Geordie!' Ah, the dulcet tones of Jackie once more.

'Yes, dear?'

'Is the tent ready yet? I want to get the bedding sorted out then I can relax.' Maybe I'm living in a parallel universe, but I could swear since we arrived, the women have been relaxing as four knuckleheads worked their nuts off under a sweltering Sun. I know better than to air my confusion.

'Nearly there, pet. Let me introduce you to farmer Clarence Longdon.' Clarence's benevolent smile morphs into a lascivious, leer. The guy gives me the screaming abdabs. He removes his hat and places it over his heart with one hand as the other hand slicks back the last remaining strands of grey, greasy hair over his bald nut. Initially, Jackie offers him a warm smile. It doesn't last long.

'Pleased to meet you,' she says with barely concealed disgust.

'And you too, my lover.' He turns and holds his arm out. 'That's my farm over yonder,' he says, pointing at a dot on the

31

horizon to the north. 'I sell organic milk, cheese, and eggs. It's on an honesty system. I'm not always around. A lot of work to do on a farm.'

'Oh,' she replies. 'That's nice to know.'

'I also have a cool room, well-hung with small-goods. Black pudding, bacon, and the finest sausage in the whole of Somerset. I call it the "Somerset Stonker". It's a whopping sausage! Biggest in the county, if not the land. If you'd like to pop around, I'll give you a free sample.' Jackie does well to hold back a dry wretch.

'Well, erm… thank you, Clarence, but we have brought a lot of food with us already, so I'm not sure we'll need to pay a visit.' The randy old git isn't giving up that easily.

'I also have an animal farm; ducks, geese, sheep, pigs. I'm sure your little ones would love to pay a visit.' She throws a glance at Geordie, who is grinning like a raving lunatic, oblivious to the dirty old man's intentions.

'Oh, so it's you who has the animal farm… I didn't realise,' Jackie murmurs.

'Aye, the kids will love it,' Geordie says. 'How about we take them up there tomorrow?'

Jackie glares at her husband. 'Ahem, yes, we'll see, Geordie,' she replies. She turns back to Clarence. 'And will your wife be around?' Clarence slumps down onto his tractor seat.

'No. I'm afraid my wife has gone.' There's stilted silence for a moment.

'I'm so sorry to hear that,' Jackie says, offering her condolences. 'How long ago did she pass away?'

Clarence appears startled. 'Oh no! She's not dead… I only wish she were. Cow! She ran off with the reticulation engineer after we'd had the septic tank emptied two years ago. Mind you, at least I didn't have to pay the bill. Last I heard, she was living in Bognor Regis. She's ditched the reticulation engineer and shacked up with the local funeral director.'

'She clearly has a taste for the high life,' I say.

'Yes… she always had stars in her eyes. Delusions of grandeur,' he adds wistfully.

'Right, well nice to meet you, Clarence, but I can hear the children fighting. I must get back,' Jackie says as desperation takes over. She turns to leave.

'Righto! See you again, my lover! And remember what I said… call around, anytime. Look for the sign on the main road— Bell End Farm!' Jackie breaks into a trot as she heads back to the laager of motorhomes and safety. Flaky, Robbo and I exchange bemused glances. Clarence returns his attention to Geordie.

'How many will be using the shithole?'

'Four of us,' Geordie replies.

'I think that's three,' Flaky corrects. 'You heard what Jackie said. And I can't say I blame her.'

Geordie glares at him. 'And what if she's caught short during the night?' He returns his gaze to the farmer. 'There'll be four of us using it.'

'Where do you want it?'

'Not too far away… but not too close either. And make sure it's downwind.' The farmer nods and smiles. I wish he wouldn't.

'Are you expecting any more campers?' Flaky asks.

'Just the one,' he replies adding no further information.

'Everywhere else is full to capacity,' I say.

'That be so.'

'How come you've only got two sets of campers?'

'This is my second year, and I haven't got around to advertising yet, apart from in the local Flexley Gazette.'

I turn to Geordie. 'How did you find this place then?'

'Like Clarence said, through the classifieds in the Flexley Gazette. That's the power of the internet. This place is half the price of anywhere else.' And therein lies the reason we're here.

'He asks a lot of questions, does your mate, doesn't he?' Clarence says peering at me with a hint of distrust.

'Don't you worry about Billy Boy, he's taciturn and suspicious by nature. He doesn't mean anything by it.'

'Hmm…' grunts Clarence. He dons his hat, starts the tractor, and heads off.

'What a character,' Geordie beams.

'What a pervert, more like,' Flaky says.

'What are you talking about! He's a friendly, old, harmless farmer. The salt of the earth. The oily handed son of toil trying to earn an honest crust in these dark and desperate times. You're no judge of character.'

'The guy's a slippery, slimy snake, a lech, a liar and to add insult to injury, and probably the worst of his crimes, a shocking dresser,' I state.

'You've changed, Bill. You've forgotten your working-class roots. It's men like old Clarence that feed this nation. Up at the crack of dawn, grafting all day until nightfall to help fill the breadbasket of this once proud nation.'

'Whatever. Come on, let's finish with this bloody tent. I've had enough for one day.'

After another thirty minutes we finally end the marathon erection. There must be at least fifty guy ropes attached to the tent. The children materialise and chase each other around the structure. It doesn't take long before Wallace goes arse over tit as he trips on a guy rope. Then Sally goes over, followed by Mary. Then Robbo trips.

'Watch where you're going, you uncoordinated idiot!' Geordie yells at Robbo before he also trips over.

'Good grief, this thing is a bloody death trap,' Flaky comments.

'It's a matter of getting used to it, that's all. Twenty-four hours from now and we won't even notice the guy ropes,' Geordie declares picking himself up as Robert goes down. 'Right, kids listen to me!' he bellows. 'Stop running around the tent. This is not a play area. It's out of bounds.' The children dutifully chase each other back towards the motorhomes. 'Bloody kids! They've got acres of empty fields to play in and they've got to play around the tent.'

'Oh, Geordie,' Jackie calls out, 'it looks wonderful. I've got to say it was worth all the effort.' I tend to disagree.

'Thank you, my love. The best things in life are worth waiting for,' he replies with pride.

'Can I get the bedding sorted out now?'

'Yes, you go for it, my love.' I flop down onto a camp chair as Geordie rearranges the barbeque. Jackie disappears into the tent with a bag full of bedding.

'I'm ready for a bottle of beer,' Robbo says as he pulls out a spliff.

'Yeah, me too,' I say.

'Better than that,' Geordie whispers, 'I think we deserve a pint or two down the local. What do you say?' He grins at us.

'Couldn't think of anything better,' I reply. 'But I'm not sure that's going to go down too well on our first night.'

'Leave it to me,' Geordie mumbles. 'I have a plan. You need to be creative in these situations.'

'Geordie!' Jackie's voice booms out.

'Oh, oh,' Robbo says. 'I know that tone and it spells trouble.'

'What's wrong, dear?' Geordie asks, as his head involuntarily twitches and a frown spreads across his face.

'Come in here a minute.' Geordie disappears inside the tent.

'I wonder what the matter is?' I whisper to Robbo, who grins at me.

'I'm not sure, but I don't think it's for a romantic romp on the inflatable mattress,' he says.

'Come on, let's take a look.' The three of us follow Geordie inside and pull back a canvas flap into the bedroom. Geordie is rubbing the back of his neck as he and Jackie stare at the wall.

'Who in hell's name is that?' Jackie demands, pointing at the portrait stencilled to the canvas.

'That's Kim Jong Un. General Secretary of the Worker's Party,' Geordie explains. She glares at him with a fearsome pout.

'And what does that stand for?' she says, pointing at the letters on the opposite flank.

'The Democratic People's Republic of Korea,' he mumbles.

'Of course, that makes sense. You've actually bought a tent from a dictator! My God! Only you could manage that. Are you friends on Facebook? Are you going to leave a review on his website?'

'Don't talk daft, woman. It's not his personal tent… well, at least I don't think it is. He wouldn't have time to go camping.'

'No, I suppose you're right. He'd be far too busy planning Armageddon. You need to cover him up. I'm not getting undressed every night in front of him!'

'He's not bloody real! It's a stencil.'

'I don't care. His eyes follow me around the room. Cover him up or you'll be sleeping in here with the boys for the week,' she yells before storming out of the tent.

*****

At last, I can put my feet up. I'm relaxing in a camping chair chatting with the women about our plans for the holiday.

'When are you going to hide the Easter eggs?' I ask Fiona.

'Once we've got the children safely into bed and we're certain they're asleep,' she explains.

'I'm not sure that's the best idea,' Jackie begins. 'I know my two boys; they'll try to keep awake as long as possible to see what's going on.'

'It's been a long day,' Julie begins. 'They've had over 7 hours in the car and been running around since we arrived. They'll be exhausted. Once we've fed them and given them a cup of cocoa, they'll be out like a light.'

'I hope you're right. I don't want my lads spoiling it for the girls by telling them the Easter Bunny isn't real.'

'Hmm…' ponders Fiona. 'I've got a better suggestion. Will and I could get up early, say about five, and hide them.'

'That's a good idea,' Gillian confirms. No, it's not! It's a terrible idea.

'Whereabouts will you hide them?' Gillian asks, scanning the barren landscape.

'Around the campervans and tents. We need to tell them it doesn't matter how many they collect, they're going to be divided up equally at the end. I don't want any tears and squabbling.' I become distracted as I glance behind me and spot Geordie emerge from his tent about twenty feet away. He's wearing nothing apart from a pair of khaki shorts and flip-flops. He picks up a toilet roll from the table, sticks it under his arm, and marches off towards the latrine.

'Hey, Robbo, look,' I say grinning at him.

'Ha ha! A man on a mission,' he chuckles. The women follow Robbo's gaze. Gillian giggles.

'For God's sake,' Jackie murmurs, covering her face. 'The man's a bloody embarrassment.'

'At least he hasn't taken the newspaper with him as Robbo does,' Julie remarks, as she throws her husband a disgusted sideways glance.

'I'm surprised, actually,' Jackie starts. 'Although, squatting over a hole is probably not conducive to reading the sport's page.' Geordie reappears after a few minutes appearing decidedly pleased with himself. He drops the toilet roll back onto the table and joins the rest of us.

'Nothing to it,' he declares. 'Drop your kegs, do your business, wipe, and cover it up with a bit of soil.'

'For God's sake, Geordie! No one wants a blow-by-blow account of your toilet habits,' Jackie fumes.

'I'm only saying, that's all. It's not difficult.'

'I hope you washed your hands,' she says as Geordie cracks open a beer.

'Of course, I did. There's a bucket of water in there with a bar of soap in it. And a towel. I've thought of everything. I planned this trip with military precision,' he explains as he puffs his chest out. He walks past me and Jackie to take up a seat. A faint smell of something foul assaults my nostrils. Jackie turns to me.

'Have you dropped one?'

'No, I bloody haven't'!' I reply, affronted at her question.

'Well, I definitely got a whiff of something disgusting. Can you smell anything, girls?'

'Such as?' Julie asks.

'I don't like to say.'

'Yes, I can smell something,' Flaky says as he sits down next to Geordie and scrunches his nose up.

'Ah, this is the life, eh?' Geordie states as he rests one leg across the other and takes a swig of beer. I stare at him, not believing what my eyes are witnessing. I tap Jackie on the arm. She turns to me.

'I think that's where the mysterious smell is coming from,' I whisper as I point at Geordie's feet. 'He's managed to curl one out onto the back of his flip-flop and squashed it in.' She shakes her head in dismay.

'Oh, my sweet giddy aunt… what next. Geordie!' she screams at him. 'You've got shite on the back of your flip-flop.'

He looks alarmed. 'What?' he says as he begins a very tentative inspection of his soiled footwear.

'You heard. You've shat on the back of your flip-flops. Get out of here and clean yourself up, you disgusting beast! And don't go inside that tent until you've disinfected yourself. In fact, you can throw the bloody flip-flops away.'

'I've just bought them,' he grumbles as he hops off towards the latrine. 'Hell, I thought I felt something sticky on my heel.' As horrified and embarrassed as Jackie is, the rest of us find it rather amusing.

5: The Arrest

I get a quick strip wash, dry myself and throw a clean top on. I emerge from the motorhome and take in the magnificent sea views. Flaky and Robbo have already joined the women around a table outside Robbo's van. The women are in a buoyant and effusive mood, which is good to see. Maybe it has something to do with the amount of white wine they've drunk. As I sit down Robbo opens a plastic cooler box and hands me a chilled beer. I crack the top and take a glug.

'Oh, yes! That is nectar,' I say. 'Where's Geordie?'

'Still getting showered, I suppose,' Robbo says.

'Talk of the devil,' I declare as I spot Geordie walking towards us. Robbo turns around and grins at him.

'Eh up! Here he comes... Chairman Kim with the shitty flip-flop.'

'Oh, hilarious!' Geordie growls.

'I hope you're all clean now,' Jackie barks at him.

'Aye, all showered and tickety-boo.'

'Where's the flip-flop?'

'In the bottom of the latrine.'

'I'm glad to hear it.'

'Can you please drop the subject,' Geordie says, clearly getting annoyed. 'It could have happened to any of us. Right, what have you girls got planned for dinner?' he asks as he gives me a sly wink. I assume his master plan, he talked about earlier, is about to be launched. The women all look at each other with vacant expressions.

'Oh, I don't feel like cooking tonight,' Julie moans.

'Nor me,' Fiona says.

'Wait! I have an idea,' Geordie replies, doing a good impersonation of the worst hammy actor in the world. 'How about fish and chips?' There's a collective chorus of "oohs" and "ahs". 'I'm ravenous and everyone loves fish and chips. We don't have to cook; we don't need any plates or cutlery. Just wrap the rubbish in the paper and put it in the bin.'

'Oh, yes, I could go fish and chips… with mushy peas,' Gillian exclaims.

'And curry sauce,' Jackie adds.

'And the kids love it too. An easy meal. Good idea, Geordie,' Fiona congratulates. Geordie stares at me, Robbo and Flaky.

'Are you boys okay with that?'

'Sounds good to me,' I reply, as Robbo nods his agreement.

'Flaky, you'll have to make do with potato cakes and chips,' Geordie says.

'No, I'm good with fish.'

'What's happened to your veganism?'

'You really amaze me! Don't you ever listen to anything I tell you?'

'Not if I can help it.'

'I haven't been a vegan for several years. I've been a vegetarian, and I recently converted. I'm now a pescatarian.'

'I thought you were Gemini?' Robbo says frowning.

'You clown! A pescatarian is a vegetarian that eats fish. My doctor advised me to introduce fish into my diet, as my iron count has been down for quite a while.'

'Good. All sorted,' Geordie says as he grabs a pencil and notepad from the table and begins taking orders. After a few minutes, he reads the list back. 'That's fifteen fish, eleven serves of chips, eight fishcakes, seven tubs of mushy peas, five tubs of curry sauce and four breadcakes.'

'And a partridge in a pear tree!' Robbo sings. Geordie rips the sheet off and holds it out to Jackie. 'And that's why we don't let you do backing vocals anymore,' he says to Robbo. 'Here you go, love. The keys are in the car. Me and the lads will keep an eye on the kids while you and the girls get the food.'

Jackie looks shocked. 'What! I can't go, neither can any of the others.'

'Come on, sweetheart, us boys have busted a ball since we arrived. It's only fair you pick up some of the slack and do the fish and chip run.'

'Oh, it's not that. We're all well over the limit. We cannae drive.' Geordie staggers sideways before he steadies himself on the back of a chair, looking shellshocked.

'Real… really?' he stammers.

'Aye,' Jackie replies. 'You and the boys will have to go.' Geordie winces like someone has stabbed him in the back of the neck with a tomahawk.

'Oh, no! Just when I thought I could put my feet up for the first time today. Now I, *and* the boys, have to trail into town to get food for everyone. Will this day never end… sweet Lord,' he says with overexaggerated weariness. 'Oh, well, needs must,' he adds rather too quickly and eagerly. 'Come on boys, let's do the food run.' I swiftly neck my beer down and follow Geordie as he strides towards the car. I'm followed by Robbo and Flaky. Geordie rubs his hands together in glee as Jackie's voice bellows out across the field.

'Geordie! It's about fifteen minutes there and fifteen minutes back. Maybe ten minutes waiting for the food. I expect you back within the hour. Don't take this as an opportunity to go for a session at the pub!'

'No, of course not, dearest. We'll only have time for a quick one. Only the one, mind. Anyway, you're not really in a position to hand out lectures about drinking, are you?' For once there's no reply from Jackie.

'I'm warning you, Geordie!' Maybe I spoke too soon. We're about to hop into the car when a "toot, toot" distracts us as an old green VW Beetle rattles down the hill.

'Oh no,' Geordie moans. 'Looks like another camper has arrived. That's all we need.'

'You surely can't complain about one other camper?' Flaky queries. 'Didn't you notice all the campsites we passed as we drove into Flexley were completely chockers?'

44

Geordie sneers at him. 'That's why I picked this site. It had no reviews, which means it's quiet. That's the way I like it. I can't be doing with strangers.'

'It is odd,' I say. 'An Easter weekend with brilliant weather and we're the only ones here. Why would that be?'

'Because I did my homework, Bill. If I had left it up to one of you three, our noses would be pressed up against someone else's backside by now.' The VW comes to a halt a few feet from us as a grey haired, older man gets out. He's wiry, average height, but looks fit and full of vim and vigour.

'Hello, my fellow campers,' he exclaims as he strides towards us holding his arm out. 'Pleased to meet you,' he says as he shakes our hands. 'I'm Bob, but my friends call me Twitchy.'

'Pleased to meet you, Bob,' Geordie says with a distinct lack of enthusiasm.

'I see you're here with your families,' he says, nodding towards the motorhomes and children who are engaged in yet another game of tig.

'Yes,' Flaky starts. 'Down here for the week. Arrived today.'

'Excellent, me too. Well, you won't see much of me.'

'And why's that?' Robbo asks.

'I'm a Twitcher.'

Robbo sports a puzzled expression. 'Is there no medication for it? They can do wonders with laser surgery these days.'

Bob laughs. 'No, I'm a bird watcher. It's my passion. I'm afraid my job is rather dreary; I'm an accountant. Five days a week behind a desk is not much fun, let me tell you.'

The next five minutes are not much fun either, as we realise that Bob is a serious contender for the most boring man on the planet award. Bob, or Twitchy as he insists we call him, recounts his encounters with buff breasted sandpipers, various warblers, gannets, and eagles of many descriptions. At one point I get an overwhelming urge to run as fast as I can and launch myself over the cliff.

'I have all my camera gear with me. I'm hoping to capture some good shots of Jack, Jack, Jack, Jack, Jack…' Oh no, the guy has a fearsome stammer that captures us off-guard. I never know how to handle these situations and always fall back to my default position of trying to guess the troublesome word. 'Jack, Jack, Jack,' he continues, stuck in a never-ending loop.

'Jack Nicholson?' Robbo offers as he leans forward with a look of concern.

'Jack, Jack, Jack…'

I can't help but offer my assistance. 'Jack Lemmon? Dempsey? Jack Black?'

'No,' Twitchy says. 'Jack, Jack, Jack…'

'Jack the Ripper?' Geordie suggests.

'No! Jack, Jack, Jack… a j, j, j, Jack Snipe!' Twitchy cries. I let out a sigh of relief. 'I also spotted Richard, Richard, Richard…' Ding, Ding! Time for round two.

'Richard Gere?' Flaky asks.

'Nixon.' Geordie says.

'No, Richard, Richard, Richard…'

'The 1st?' I say.

'Branson? Little Richard? Cliff Richard?' Robbo pleads with him with desperation in his eyes.

'Rich, Rich, Rich, r... r.... Richard's Pipit!' he exclaims much to everyone's delight. I need a lie down, I feel quite exhausted.

'Right, well, that's nice to know. Would love to stop and chat some more but we're heading into town to get fish and chips. The kids will get cranky if they're not fed soon,' I say as I open the car door. The others follow suit.

'I fully understand. We can catch up later for a chinwag. I'll pitch my tent well away from you. Don't want to invade your space.' I smile at him as Geordie starts the engine, and the car moves away.

'Thank Christ for that,' Geordie says as he wipes a bead of sweat from his brow. 'That was worse than a game of charades with the kids.'

*****

As we enter the outskirts of Flexley-on-Sea, Geordie jabs his elbow into my arm.

'You see what I did back there, with the women?' he says as he turns to me, grinning.

'Yep, I saw what you did. Keep your eyes on the road.'

'You need to plant the seed, then let them pick it up and run with it,' he explains, suffering from an acute case of the mixed metaphors. 'If I say so myself, it was a masterful display of lateral thinking. You need to start with your goal then work backwards.'

'That's not lateral thinking,' Flaky corrects. 'That's reverse thinking.'

'Don't split hairs!' Geordie barks. 'The outcome is the same.'

'Hey, dead ahead! The "Battered Fryer". And it has a line of customers queuing up, always a good sign,' I say, pointing at the fish and chip shop.

'And even better,' Geordie begins, 'two doors down, The Railway Inn. Perfect. I love it when a plan comes together.' We park up opposite the chippy and amble our way across the road. Geordie pulls out the list of food orders.

'Wow! This place is popular,' Flaky says as we join the back of the line, which stretches a good twenty feet down the street.

'Here you go, Flaky,' Geordie says as he thrusts the order into his hand. 'No point all four of us queuing up. We'll be in the Railway. I'll get you a pint in.'

'Hang on! Why am I the one that's got to queue up?'

'That's the problem with you; it's all about self, self, self. Don't you think me, Robbo, and Will deserve a slight respite? Stop being so egoistic and think about others for a change!' he yells back.

The pub is relatively quiet, much to Geordie's pleasure.

'Evening gentlemen, what can I get you?' the barman asks as Geordie leans against the counter.

'Four pints of bitter and three whisky chasers… in fact, make those doubles.'

The barman laughs. 'You boys had a hard day?' he replies as he dispenses the whisky.

'You could say that,' Robbo comments. We each pick up the whisky glasses and hold them aloft.

'Boys, here's to the start of *our* holiday. Cheers!' Geordie declares. We smash the whisky back in one hit and pick up our beers. 'Down in one, lads.' Geordie slams his empty pint onto the bar in seconds, while Robbo and I take a tad longer. 'Your shout, Robbo,' he declares. Robbo finishes his pint, wipes the suds from his top lip and orders three more beers as I finish the dregs of my first one. With glasses refilled, we all wander outside to the beer garden and spark up. A flyer, pinned to the back of the door, diverts Geordie's attention.

'Hey, look at this,' he says. 'It's an arm-wrestling competition in a few days' time. A couple of local Somerset heroes called "Nutmeg and Ginger" invite all-comers to try their luck against them. £20 per go to win £200. I'll be having some of that! What have I got to lose?'

'£20,' Robbo says. 'Or probably *my* £20!'

Geordie glares at him. 'Oh, shut up you tightwad! You'll get your money back. Keep a tab on everything and when we get back home, we'll divvy everything up.'

'I've heard that before,' Robbo mumbles. I stub my cigarette into the ashtray.

'Come on, let's head back inside, Flaky might be looking for us. I'm absolutely famished. Let's get back to the campground.'

'Steady on, Bill. Surely we can fit in one more?' Geordie says as he swallows the rest of his pint. The alcohol has already kicked in and I'm feeling slightly exuberant.

'Okay, but only one more, and that's it, right?'

'Aye. Just the one,' Geordie beams. Back in the main bar, I order another three pints as Flaky walks in looking glum. Geordie hands him a pint.

'I didn't want a drink,' he complains.

'Too late, sunshine, I got you one.' Flaky reluctantly takes it and takes a genteel sip.

'Do you know how much that bloody fish and chip order cost? No wonder you all abandoned me. It cost...' Geordie cuts him off.

'I don't know what's wrong with you and Robbo. Here we are on holiday, and all you two can do is gripe about the cost of things. Chill out, relax. Who cares about money? What's the waiting time for the fish and chips?' he adds, deftly changing the conversation.

'About fifteen minutes,' Flaky replies, sulkily.

'Excellent!' Geordie exclaims. 'Time for another couple.' Christ! We're already onto our third pint within twenty minutes... not to mention the double whisky chaser. 'Another three pints of bitter,' Geordie says, turning towards the bar. The barman gets new pint glasses and pulls at the pump.

I peer at Robbo. 'Feeling pissed yet?'

'Getting there, fast. Too fast!'

'Hey, this arm-wrestling contest you've got advertised, what's the go?' Geordie quizzes as the barman places the first pint down on the bar.

'Couple of local boys, twins. They're farmhands, short but stocky. Both built like brick shithouses. Every holiday season they do the arm wrestle comp. We get a lot of out-of-towners this time of year… like you guys. Some drink too much and reckon they can take them on. Never been beaten yet.'

'Is that right?' Geordie says.

'Yep. Undisputed champions of Somerset.'

'Aye, but Somerset is a small place compared to the rest of the world.' The barman places the second pint down and chuckles.

'That's what they all say. As I said, never been beaten. You boys staying local?'

'Aye, at Farmer Clarence's campsite a few miles out of town,' Geordie replies. The barman throws an enigmatic smile as he pulls the last pint.

'Ah, Farmer Clarence. You boys watch your wallet's while Clarence is around, otherwise, he'll empty it faster than you can say, Jack Robinson. He's a crafty one, is old Clarence.'

We chitchat idly with the barman for another ten minutes until Geordie notices the clock on the wall.

'Flaky, you need to get back to the chippy and collect the food. Hey, give Gillian a ring and tell her we're running a bit late because of the queues, or no doubt I'll get the blame when we get back.'

'Any more orders, Herr Kapitan?' Flaky grumbles as he finishes his drink and leaves the pub.

'I'm smashed,' Robbo mumbles.

'I'm feeling lightheaded myself,' I agree.

'Come on boys, get it down you. Time for one more before Old Mother Hen returns.'

Flaky is soon back with two plastic carrier bags bulging at the seams.

'Come on,' he says, 'let's get going.'

'Hold your horses. We've just got refills. Here, I got you another,' Geordie says as he hands Flaky a pint.

'I didn't bloody want one!' he protests.

'You can be an ungrateful sod at times,' Geordie says, looking mortally wounded. Flaky relents as he puts the bags down and takes the drink.

'Sorry. I'm not ungrateful. I'm tired and hungry,' he says, taking a sip of beer.

'Apology accepted. That's the sort of man I am. Did you ring Gillian?'

'Yes. I told her we'd be about twenty minutes.'

'Good man. Right, sup up, don't want to let the fish and chips go cold.' Flaky struggles manfully to neck his pint down in one, but it takes him four attempts. We wait for him at the entrance. 'Come on, Flaky! You're holding the show up,' Geordie chides. Flaky puts his empty glass down and we make our way outside. As we head towards the car, Geordie pulls the keys from his pocket.

'Here, you better drive,' he says, passing Flaky the keys. 'Better safe than sorry.'

Flaky is aghast. 'But... I've had two pints. I'll be over the limit.'

'Don't talk soft, wee man. You're allowed two pints in the first hour and one pint per hour thereafter and you'll still be under the legal limit.' Flaky turns to Robbo and me.

'Is that true?' he asks.

'Technically… yes,' Robbo confirms. Flaky seems appeased and jumps into the driver's seat. We set off at a sedate pace as we leave Flexley and climb the coastal road back to the campsite. Five minutes out of town Geordie turns around and stares out of the back window.

'Coppers 6 o'clock,' he states. Flaky glances nervously in the rearview mirror.

'Yes, he's been behind us since we left Flexley. Robbo, when you said "technically" what exactly did you mean?'

'About how much you could drink?'

'Yes.'

'The two-pint theory is a ballpark figure. It all depends on your height, weight, and metabolism. Oh, and the last time you ate and how tired you are.'

'Just great!' Flaky spits. 'I haven't eaten since this morning and I'm dead on my feet.'

'You'll be fine,' Geordie reassures him. 'Anyway, what are you mithering about? The coppers haven't even pulled you over yet,' he says as a quick blast of a police siren sounds out.

'Shit!' Flaky yells as he manoeuvres the car to the side of the road. We turn around to witness a solitary police officer emerge from his vehicle and stride towards us. He taps on the driver's window. Flaky winds it down.

'Evening, sir,' the copper says as he peers at us suspiciously, as they tend to do.

'Evening officer,' Flaky replies, bearing a strained smile.

'Do you realise your driver's side brake light is not working?'

Geordie leans across. 'Oh, aye. Sorry about that, officer. I noticed it this morning but haven't had a chance to get it fixed yet.' The copper appears confused.

'Is this your vehicle?' he asks Flaky.

'No,' Geordie interrupts again. 'It's my car, officer, but don't worry. My insurance lets anyone drive it as long as they're over twenty-five.' The police officer nods thoughtfully.

'I see. You boys holidaying down here?'

'Yes,' Flaky begins. 'We're camping at Farmer Longdon's place on top of the hill.'

'Old Longdon, eh? He's finally snared some customers,' the officer chuckles. 'Keep your eye on him,' he adds, cryptically.

'What do you mean?' Flaky asks.

'He's known around these parts as Longdon Silver, and for good reason. Always up to mischief. Let's just say he's a sharp operator,' he adds tapping his nose.

'You could never accuse him of being a sharp dresser,' I comment from the back. It falls completely flat. Not so much as a giggle. The copper appears to have lost interest in proceedings.

'Make sure you get the brake light fixed as soon as you can. If I stop you again, I won't be as lenient.'

'Aye, no problem officer. I'll sort it out first thing Tuesday morning,' Geordie says.

'Yes, thank you…' Flaky begins. He doesn't get any further as he emits an involuntary burp. The officer, who was probably hoping to make a quick exit and put his feet up at the station, takes an exaggerated step back. His eyes narrow.

'Been drinking, sir?'

'Erm, ye… yes,' Flaky stammers as he throws Geordie a nervous glance.

'How many?'

'Just the, erm… just the two… pints.'

'I'm afraid I'll need to breathalyse you. I won't be a minute.' The copper heads back to the patrol car.

'Christ!' Flaky hisses. 'This is all your fault, Geordie!'

'How do you work that out?'

'Forcing beer on me when I didn't want it,' he snaps back angrily.

'Hang on sunshine, you're a grown man. I cannae make you do anything you don't want to. If you're reckless enough to get behind the wheel of a car after you've been drinking, you only have yourself to blame.' I think Flaky's head is about to self-combust.

'You handed me the damn keys!'

'You didn't have to take them. Anyway, look on the bright side.'

'What bloody bright side?'

'If it had been me driving, they'd have locked me up and thrown away the keys. At least you have a fighting chance.' The policeman returns and holds the breathalyser as Flaky blows into it. The copper stares at it for a moment, his face showing no emotion.

'I'm sorry, sir, but this reading is telling me you're slightly over the limit.'

'But I can't be! I only had two pints. You can't be over the limit with two drinks!'

'Technically,' Robbo mutters from the back.

'That's an urban myth,' says the copper. 'There're many factors involved. It's not as simple as that.'

Robbo leans forward. 'I believe he has the statutory right to request a blood or urine sample,' he says. The policeman cocks his head and huffs.

'That's correct, sir. Although it means coming down to the station and requesting a doctor to come out and perform the test. It's not cheap, and the defendant bears the cost.'

'Defendant! Holy smoke! I've been tried and convicted already,' Flaky squawks, becoming ever more distraught.

'Robbo's right,' Geordie states. 'Get yourself down to the station for a blood test. Those breathalyser machines are unreliable.'

'It's your prerogative, sir,' says the copper.

'Yes… yes, that's what I'll do. Am I under arrest?'

'No, of course you're not under arrest!' Geordie scoffs. 'You're merely assisting the police with their inquiries,' he adds with a chuckle.

'It's not bloody funny!' We all troop out of the car.

'Excuse me, officer, but I don't suppose there's any chance of a lift to our campground? We have a fish and chip supper for our wives and children, and it will be cold if we have to walk back,' I ask, sporting my most hopeful expression. Much to my surprise, the police officer reluctantly agrees.

'I suppose so. It's not something I make a habit of though.'

'Thank you. It's much appreciated.'

'Flaky, as the accused, you best sit upfront,' Geordie says as he opens the back door of the police car and we all pile in. He leans forward and whispers into the copper's ear. 'If I were you, officer, I'd be putting handcuffs on the suspect. He has a reputation as a bolter.'

'Will you shut your bloody gob!' Flaky fires back.

'No need for the handcuffs. I don't think he's going anywhere,' the copper replies.

The patrol car pulls into the campsite and rolls slowly down the hill. The women are all sitting in the same positions as when we left them well over an hour ago. As we near, they all jump to their feet and gawp in horror at the police car. I thrust my head out of the window and wave.

'Don't worry, we're all okay,' I shout.

'Aye, nothing to be alarmed about,' Geordie yells as he sticks his head out the other side. 'Flaky's been arrested for drink driving, that's all!' As the car comes to a halt Geordie grabs the fish and chips and jumps out. 'Come on everybody, grub up! Flaky, I'll put yours on a plate and keep it warm for you in the oven.'

'Thanks,' he whispers as he stares out of the window with teary eyes. I slap him on the shoulder as I alight from the car.

'Keep your pecker up, Flaky. I'm sure the blood test will be negative. You'll be back here in no time.'

'Do you really think so?' he murmurs.

'Yes, of course I do,' I reply as Gillian rushes towards the car.

'And if you're not, the cells in modern police stations are quite comfortable these days,' Robbo adds.

*****

'They were the best fish and chips I've ever had,' Robbo announces as he leans back in his chair and takes a glug of beer.

'Aye, well worth the effort. And nothing to clean up,' Geordie says as he scrunches the paper up and throws it into a black bin liner at the side of the motorhome.

We shower the exhausted children, get them into their pyjamas and tuck them up in bed. I read a bedtime story to Mary but within a few minutes, her eyes close. I kiss her tenderly on the head.

'Night, night, sweetpea. Daddy loves you.' I'm feeling quite tired myself. I go back outside and grab a glass of red wine as a nightcap.

'Hey, look, it's the Range Rover,' Fiona declares. We all stare up the hill as the car snakes its way towards us.

'It must be Flaky,' Gillian says as she leaps from her chair. The car pulls up and Flaky jumps out sporting the biggest grin.

'What happened?' his wife asks as she flings her arms around him as though he's just completed a twenty stretch in Wandsworth.

'When we got to the station, the police officer, Sergeant Waygood, gave me another breath test prior to contacting a doctor. Apparently, the machine at the station is a lot more sophisticated and reliable. I blew slightly under, so he released me. He even gave me a lift back to the car. He's a very nice chap.'

'There you go!' Geordie says. 'All's well that ends well. But let that be a lesson to you. Drink driving is a mug's game. You're a menace to yourself and the public at large. Now, take a seat and put your feet up. I'll get your fish and chips for you.' Flaky sits at the table and lets out a sigh of relief. Geordie's back in a jiffy, clutching two plates covering each other. He's sporting an enormous pair of oven mitts. 'Here you go, tuck in,' he encourages as he places the food in front of Flaky and carefully removes the top plate. The fish and chips are withered to a fraction of their former glory. Flaky taps at the fish with his fork. It's as hard as rock.

'Wonderful,' he mutters, unhappily.

'What temperature did you set the oven to?' Jackie snaps at her husband.

'280, as you said.'

'I said, about 80, cloth ears!'

6: The Goose

Fiona jabs me in the ribs with her elbow.

'Ow! What's that for?'

'Shush. You'll wake Mary. It's Sunday.'

'I know it's Sunday. You don't need to wake me up to tell me what bloody day it is,' I grumble.

'No, it's Easter Sunday.'

'Crap and shit,' I moan as I remember Fiona has kindly nominated herself and me to get up early to hide the Easter eggs.

'Don't be like that. You should savour these moments. Once they're gone, they'll be gone for good. They're not children forever, you know.'

'Not only do you volunteer me to do things, without running it by me first, but then you wake me up at five in the morning and lay a guilt trip on me.'

'Stop your moaning, you grump. Come on, it'll be fun.' I sit up in bed and stare out of the window.

'Not my idea of fun. It's still bloody dark outside.' Fiona has already slipped into a pair of jogging pants and a loose top. I also note that she's not wearing a bra and I'm suffering from a severe case of the morning glories. 'Hey, Fi?'

'What?' she whispers.

'How about you and me find a quiet spot outside and, you know…'

'You gotta be joking. How can you think of sex so early in the morning?'

I rub the back of my neck. 'My penis doesn't care what the time is. It's a law unto itself. Little Billy is always willing to serve.'

'Tell Little Billy, from me, the only service he'll be getting today is self-service. Now hurry and get dressed. I'll put the kettle on and make us a cuppa before we start.' She closes the door gently behind her as I lift the blankets up and stare at my old friend.

'Sorry, pal. I tried my best.'

We take about fifteen minutes to hide the Easter eggs. We place dozens of small ones around the campervans and Geordie's tent, hidden on window openings, on top of gas bottles and under tables. We strategically place the large ones in the middle of the field in five nests of straw. Fiona had the foresight to write names on each egg to stop any squabbles. When we're done, we sit back in our camp chairs with a cup of tea and a plate of buttered toast. The Sun is rising in the east as we enjoy the tranquil solitude.

'It's a lovely spot,' Fiona murmurs as she stares out at the murky waters of the Bristol Channel.

'It is. I'm still concerned about the cliffs.'

She smiles at me. 'You're such a worrywart, aren't you? We've warned the children to keep in the field unless they're with an adult. They're not babes who go wandering off. They're a sensible bunch… on the whole.'

61

'Hmm...'

'And what does that mean?'

'Wallace is a worry.'

'He's not that bad.'

'No, he's not bad. But unfortunately, he's inherited his father's "idiot" gene. He does things on the spur of the moment without thinking of the consequences.' I glance at my watch and for a moment consider going back to bed until a more pressing matter raises its head. I stare at the shower tent at the back of the campervan. 'Hey, Fi?'

'Yes?'

I nod towards the shower. 'What do you think?'

'Come off it, Will. You can't be that desperate.'

'It's been a long time between drinks.'

'It's four days ago since we last had sex.'

'Exactly! Well?' She looks at the tent, then back to me, and at the tent again. This is a promising development.

'Okay, I suppose... but it will have to be a quickie and no noise.' I leap from my chair and rub my hands together.

'Daddy, what day is it?' I love my daughter more than life itself and there's no greater feeling than to witness her little innocent face each morning as she rises from her sleep. But... sometimes... her timing is lousy.

'It's Sunday, sweetpea,' I sigh as I see my early morning nookie evaporate into thin air.

'Easter Sunday?'

'Yes.' Her eyes become as wide as dinner plates.

'Has the Easter Bunny been?' she asks with an air of eager expectancy.

'I'm not sure. You better wake the others up, grab your Easter baskets and go on an Easter egg hunt.' She scurries off to Robbo and Julie's van and knocks on the door.

'Sally, Sally, wake up. I think the Easter Bunny has been.' I turn to Fiona who is smiling sweetly at me.

'Thwarted at every turn,' I murmur.

'Don't worry. It's not the end of the world.' I beg to differ. The crack of gunshots in the distance distracts me. 'Was that a gun I heard?' Fiona says, looking troubled. Another two blasts ring out.

'Yeah. Probably a farmer out shooting foxes.'

'God, I hate those things.'

'Foxes?'

'No, silly. Guns. They're nothing but trouble.'

It's not long before all five children are running around excitedly collecting up chocolate eggs and depositing them in their baskets. The other women and Flaky soon join us. Amazingly, despite the screeching and shrill squeals of laughter, Robbo, and Geordie sleep on through. Lazy gets!

I'm busy in the camp kitchen cooking pancakes when I hear two high-pitched screams coming from behind Geordie's tent. I race to see what's going on. Mary and Katrina are in a state of rigid shock as they stare at Farmer Clarence and what he's holding in his hands.

Clarence has a shotgun, uncocked, resting over his shoulder. In his grasp are two dead rabbits, held aloft by their ears. Wallace arrives on the scene, panting hard.

'Shit the bed! The farmer's shot the Easter Bunny and its wife,' he exclaims with a certain amount of ironic glee. The girls begin to sob.

*****

I'm driving the motorhome with Robbo and Flaky sat alongside. Geordie is ahead, in the Range Rover, with the children. His car slows and indicates right.

'There's the sign,' Robbo says. 'Bell End Farm.'

'A rather unfortunate name,' Flaky mutters. 'You'd have thought someone would have had a quiet word with him.' We follow Geordie up a dirt track, for a mile or so, until we arrive at a large, dilapidated farmhouse.

'Christ,' I murmur. 'This place has seen better days.' The house is in desperate need of a lick of paint and a glazier. Various pieces of rusty farm machinery litter the driveway. There are two barns next to the house. One is leaning at a precarious angle. Weeds and long grass poke out from the gutters. A knackered old sign that reads "Farm Shop" is nailed to the door. 'So, this is the Lothario's lair.'

'You can understand why he's got to fight women off with a shitty stick,' Robbo says. We jump from the van as the three girls emerge from the Range Rover. They run around excitedly and clap their hands together as Geordie opens the boot. Wallace and Robert scamper out of the rear seats and join the girls in animated anticipation. Geordie wanders over to us.

'My God! I drew the short straw. Those girls never stop talking and asking questions. My ears are bleeding.'

'Make the most of it, mate. Once they hit puberty all you'll get is pouts, silence, and filthy looks,' I reply as the door to the farmhouse creaks open. Out walks Clarence, looking like he's had a massive night on the piss. Same dirty white shirt and pants held up by string.

'Ah, it's the happy campers. You've brought the kiddies to see the animal farm?'

'Yes. They've been nagging all morning,' Geordie replies as Mary and Katrina edge behind me and Flaky. Their trauma, from the early morning execution of the Easter Bunny, still lingers despite being told repeatedly the farmer had shot two hares, not the Easter Bunny and his soulmate. Clarence smiles at them.

'I'm sorry about earlier, girls. But hares are a pest to farmers. I promise you… it was not the Easter Bunny.' He goes to pat them on the head, but Katrina and Mary fall further back behind me and Flaky, grabbing at our trousers. 'My! They're bonny looking girls. Are they twins?'

Mary responds indignantly. 'No! I'm sick of people saying that!' Robbo and Geordie throw me an embarrassed glance.

'Well, if you're not twins, you certainly sprouted from the same flower bed.' The girls have no idea what he's on about. Flaky steps forward and places his palm on Katrina's head.

'Not at all. This one, Katrina, is mine. And this little scamp is Will's daughter,' he explains with good-natured kindliness as he gently rubs his knuckles on Mary's head. Farmer Clarence eyes me inquisitively, then stares at Flaky for a moment before he raises one bushy eyebrow and nods.

'Oh, I see. Okay, follow me. The animal farm is in a small paddock at the back of the house.' Sally and the boys run up to him as the rest of us follow.

'What's your name?' Sally asks.

'You can call me Farmer Clarence,' he replies.

'Why?' Robert says.

'Because I'm a farmer and my first name is Clarence.'

'My dad's a musician, but he's not called Musician Geordie. He's just called Geordie. Although, my mum sometimes calls him other things.'

Clarence chuckles. 'I didn't invent the name. It's what folks around here call me. I guess it's a sort of nickname.'

'What animals have you got?' Wallace says. Clarence opens a gate at the side of the farmhouse as we follow him down a narrow gravel path.

'There's a farrow of pigs, rabbits, a few lambs, and some geese with a clutch of chicks,' he replies in a cheery tone.

'Aren't baby geese called goslings?' Sally quizzes.

'That's right,' Clarence responds with a warm smile that flashes his blackened molars at her. Her eyes widen as she drops from his side and grabs Robbo's hand. 'Here we are. Now, all the kiddies can go in but only two adults. The geese are a little overprotective of their young. Children don't seem to bother them but if they get too many adults in their space, they can get aggressive.'

'I'll go in,' Geordie states. 'I have an affinity with animals.'

'I'll join you,' Flaky says.

'That's £5, please,' Clarence says.

'That's very reasonable,' Geordie comments, smiling.

'Per child,' Clarence adds.

'Ah, I see. Robbo, do the honours, will you?'

'Why don't you put your hand in your pocket for once?'

'I've told you… I don't have any cash on me.'

'Very convenient.' Robbo extracts his wallet, pulls out the notes, and hands them to Clarence who quickly grabs them as he opens the gate to the paddock.

'Clarence, while we're here we thought we'd buy some provisions from you,' I say.

'Excellent! Follow me back to the barn.'

As ramshackle as the barn appears from the outside, inside it's clean and functional, if not spotless. A row of old fridges and a box freezer line the back wall. Cured meats hang from the rafters and neatly stacked boxes of eggs sit on a wooden table.

'What you after?' Clarence says.

'We'll take five pounds of streaky bacon, two dozen eggs, and have you any sausages?'

'In the fridge,' he says as he starts up the bacon slicer and drops a side of bacon onto it. Robbo inspects the fridge.

'Is it pork or beef sausage?' Robbo calls out above the whine of the slicing machine.

'The short fat ones are pork and the great big, long ones are my famous beef Somerset Stonkers.' Robbo glances at me. As much as I hate to eat a sausage called the "Somerset Stonker" made by Clarence's own fair hand, I'm not a fan of pork sausage.

'Beef,' I say to Robbo. He pulls out a pack of ridiculously long, fat sausages.

'Christ,' Robbo mutters, 'you could do some damage with these buggers.' As he's about to close the door, he stops and grabs a block of cheese. He smiles and beckons me over. He holds it out in front of him. 'What do you reckon, fancy a nice slab of Bell End Cheese? Go nice with a plate of crackers.'

I chuckle. 'I'm going to struggle putting a Somerset Stonker in my mouth, but I draw the line at eating Bell End Cheese.'

'How about we get a block for Flaky?'

'Good idea. He's a cheese nut.' Clarence turns off the machine and wraps the bacon. 'You all musicians?' he asks.

'Yeah.'

'You in a band together?' he asks, looking guardedly at me.

'Yes. The Shooting Tsars,' I reply.

'The Shooting Stars… never heard of you,' he says with an element of contempt. I long ago gave up on correcting people about the band name.

'Ever heard of U2 or Coldplay?'

'Nah, can't say I have. Last band I went to see was The Troggs at the Pavilion in Flexley. 1973, or was it '74? That'll be £23, all up,' he says as he deposits the sausage, bacon, eggs, and cheese into a plastic carrier bag. He hands the bag over as I pass him a twenty and a ten. He fumbles in his pocket with a pained expression. 'I'm afraid I don't have any change.'

'Don't worry,' I say. I notice a pile of business cards on his counter and pick one up.

'Robbo, fancy a spot of fishing?' I say as I hand him the card.

'Aquatherapy Fishing Charters,' Robbo says as he reads the card. 'I suppose it could be fun. How far does it go out?'

'Oh, not far. Just off the coast of Flexley,' Clarence says. 'We don't take children, though. Got to be over sixteen.'

'Even better,' Robbo grins. 'A few hours peace and quiet.'

'I can book you in if you want?'

'Oh, you take bookings, do you?' I say, a little confused.

'It's my boat. I don't go out myself. I employ a skipper, Bubbles, he runs the show.'

'You've got a few things on the go,' Robbo says. 'A farm, a shop, homemade produce, a fishing charter, and an animal farm.'

'I like to keep busy. The devil makes work for idle hands. What day do you want to go?' I look at Robbo.

'Can't do Monday as we're going to the funfair. Tuesday we're at the aqua park. Wednesday is a walk and a picnic on the beach.'

'Hell, you've got it all mapped out,' Robbo says, looking impressed.

'Not me, mate. The women had it all pre-planned. They could organise an invasion of a small country, on the back of an envelope, in about ten minutes. Righto, Clarence, book the four of us for Thursday morning. What time and where?'

'6 am, harbour wall.'

'Hang on a mo,' Robbo begins. 'Did you say, 6 am?'

'Yes, why? You can start earlier if you want.'

'Earlier! I was thinking of later, like maybe 2 pm.'

Clarence laughs. 'Early morning is the best time to catch fish. You'll be back onshore by midday.'

'6 am will be fine,' I say. 'How much do we owe you?'

'It's £60 per head.' I pull my wallet out again and hand over more notes, which Clarence greedily accepts.

'Much obliged. Right, I have work to do. See yourselves out and remember to shut the gate on the paddock to the animal farm.'

We stash the food in the campervan's fridge and head back to the others.

'That copper was right about Old Clarence; he is a bloody sharp operator,' Robbo comments. 'We haven't been here a day, and he's winkled over a grand out of us.'

'As Geordie says, it's only money.'

'Aye, rarely his own though.'

We lean against the gate to the animal farm and peruse the scene.

'Look at that knobhead,' I say, nodding at Geordie in disbelief as Robbo sparks up a spliff and shakes his head as he inhales.

'I do believe he's a successful experiment in artificial stupidity.'

'Geordie,' I call out as he leads the children towards the geese and their goslings like the Pied Piper. 'Don't get too close. You heard what Clarence said. They can be very protective of their young.' Geordie stops and turns to me.

'Don't you worry, Bill. I know a thing or two about animal psychology,' he shouts back.

'Since when did he know anything about animal psychology?' Robbo says, puzzled, as he puffs a plume of smoke into the air.

'Probably when he was at school, same as all the other things he's an expert in.'

'I can see him in a safari suit scouring the back streets of Glasgow in a pith helmet.'

'I don't think they make pith helmets that big. Geordie! That male goose is becoming very aggressive,' I warn as he and the kids unwittingly chaperone the geese into a corner of the paddock. 'You're trapping them!' I shout as the geese honk, violently.

'Listen, Bill, leave it to me. I know what I'm doing. The thing with wild animals is that it's all about bluster. If an animal charges, all you need to do is stand your ground. They'll run right up to you and stop dead in their tracks once they realise you're not intimidated. You've got to look them straight in the eye... let them know who's boss. Humans are top of the food chain for a reason. Come on kids, nice and slow and no sudden movements or shouting.' The children appear a lot more tentative than Geordie, mind you, individually they have a lot more common sense. The goose and gander flex their wings belligerently as they hiss.

'Kids!' I call out. 'Don't go any further. Flaky, can you walk them back to the gate?'

'Will do. Come on children, make your way to the gate,' Flaky calls out with some urgency. Geordie throws me a dismissive look.

'For God's sake, Bill! Do you want these kids growing up scared of their own shadows?'

'No, only aggressive geese and deranged Scotsmen.'

'Weak as piss!' he cries with disdain. The geese give one more warning shot across the bows. Their enormous wings flap erratically as they emit deafening honks followed by angry hissing. Flaky shepherds the children to safety and closes the gate behind him. The larger goose has had enough of a six-and-a-half-foot, lumbering, Scottish oaf threatening his progeny, and takes off down the hill with its neck low and straight. Geordie stands up tall, chest puffed out. He throws a quick glance over his shoulder at us, smiles and winks. As he has his back to me, I cannot initially tell what part of his body receives the full brunt of the attack. His cries of anguish soon inform me.

'Jesus H Christ! My fucking cock!' He spins around and pelts towards the gate as the goose bears down on him for another go. In a rare feat of athleticism, he dives over the gate and lands in a heap on the ground. The goose stops, hisses then retreats up the paddock. 'It got me right on the end of my bobby's helmet. The vindictive, vicious bastard,' he groans, clutching at his groin. The children appear to be in a profound state of shock.

'I wonder if that's why it's called Bell End Farm?' Robbo chortles.

'It's not bloody funny!'

'I beg to differ,' Robbo replies, wiping a tear from his eye.

7: The Swelling

The bacon, sausages, and eggs are sizzling on the barbeque manned by Robbo. I'm standing next to him, keeping a close eye on proceedings as I sip on a cup of tea. Fiona and Gillian are setting out plates and cutlery on the table as Julie washes up pots. Jackie exits her tent.

'How's the patient?' Fiona asks.

Jackie grimaces. 'Oh, he's all right, apart from his incessant moaning. It's his old fellow I'm worried about.' I exchange a sly smile with Robbo.

'What's wrong with it?' Gillian says.

'It's all swollen and angry looking,' she replies. I snort tea down my nose.

'No different to normal, then,' Julie remarks with a wicked grin.

'Take advantage of it while you can,' Fiona begins. 'We'll plate you up some food and keep it warm.'

'You've got to be joking,' Jackie says, trying to suppress a smile. 'It's like a baby's arm that's been caught in a mangle. He won't let me near it.'

'First time for everything,' Gillian adds.

'I've told him, if the swelling hasn't gone down in an hour, then he needs to see a doctor.' Robbo pushes the bacon and sausage to one side as I scoop the eggs onto a plate.

'Okay everyone, grub up!' I shout.

'I'll see if Geordie wants any,' Jackie says as she heads back to her tent. Robbo drops the bacon and huge Stonker sausages onto another plate, and we make our way to the table.

'Tuck in everybody,' I say as Flaky emerges from his campervan carrying two cooked veggie burgers. He sits down opposite Gillian as Jackie returns.

'Geordie will be here in a moment,' she says as she takes a seat and dishes out the food. 'Please don't make any jokes about it. He's not in a good mood,' she says, specifically looking at me and Robbo.

'Jackie! I'm appalled you'd think such a thing. I can assure you, as a man, there's nothing funny about getting a bite to your bald-headed-sailor.'

'Will's right,' Robbo says. 'I wouldn't wish a bruised spam javelin on my worst enemy. Eh up, here he comes now. Herman von Longschlongstein.' We all spin around to watch. Pain and misery are etched into Geordie's face. He limps along, bow legged, in a pair of old baggy football shorts.

'Come on, Geordie, get some grub into you. It will make you feel better,' I say, offering him encouragement. He sits tentatively at the end of the table as Jackie hands him a plate of bacon and eggs and a mug of tea.

'Have you taken any painkillers?' Fiona inquires with a concerned air which does well to hide her amusement.

Geordie nods. 'Aye. Two paracetamol and two ibuprofen. Thanks for your concern, Fiona. I'm glad to see someone is taking the matter seriously. I've had scant sympathy from my dear wife and only mockery and lectures from my "so-called" friends,' he says scowling at Robbo and me, then finally at Flaky.

'I guess it comes with the territory,' Flaky states as he bites into his veggie burger, topped with Bell End Cheese.

'What territory?' Geordie mumbles as he stares at his plate.

Flaky grins. 'Being an expert in animal psychology. Birds are renowned for attacking people. Those geese gave you plenty of warnings.' Geordie ignores him. I pull the plate of sausages into the middle of the table.

'My God!' exclaims Jackie. 'Look at the size of those bangers.'

'Does it remind you of anything?' Julie sniggers. Jackie bites down on her lip.

'Jackie's right though, Geordie. If the swelling hasn't gone down in an hour, you best see the quack,' I say. He throws me a withering glance, unsure if my reference was deliberate or not. I keep a straight face. 'If it gets infected, you could get gangrene. You may lose it.'

'What do you mean; lose it?'

'Amputation,' I add as I slice neatly through a Somerset Stonker and jab one end with my fork. I hold it up towards Geordie. 'Stonker?' His eyes narrow to slits as he shakes his head.

'No thanks. I'll give it a miss,' he grumbles as he pokes and prods at his food.

'How's the Bell End Cheese?' Robbo asks, turning to Flaky.

'It's surprisingly good. Moist, soft, and creamy. Not dissimilar to Camembert. It does initially have a slightly peculiar taste.'

'I might try some later. I'm quite partial to a plate of cheese and quackers,' Robbo says.

'Very funny. I hope you choke on it,' Geordie growls.

'Ooh, what's wrong with these three madams,' Gillian notes as Mary, Sally, and Katrina trudge towards us with downcast faces and severe pouts.

'What's the matter, girls?' Jackie asks.

'It's not fair,' Sally says, stamping her foot and crossing her arms.

'What's not fair?' I say.

'It's Wallace and Robert,' declares Mary. 'All they want to do is play tig and we're sick of it. They won't play anything else.'

'Is that right! We'll see about that. Wallace, Robert! Get your backsides up here right now!' Jackie bellows, deafening everyone around the table. The boys know better than to answer back and are soon standing in front of their mother being lectured. 'Let the girls pick something to play for a change. They're sick of playing tig. You can't pick the games *all* the time.'

'That's right,' I say. 'What's good for the goose is good for the gander.'

'We've asked them what they want to play, but they can never agree on anything,' Wallace pleads his case.

'How about a game of, what's the time, Mr Fox? You all like that,' I suggest. The girls appear unsure.

'Or maybe, duck, duck, goose. That's always fun,' Robbo chuckles.

'Yes! duck, duck, goose!' The girls yelp as they run off. The two boys pull faces but reluctantly follow.

'Ooh, that breeze is fresh,' Gillian says as she pulls a cardigan from the back of her chair and slips it on.

'It is,' Robbo agrees. 'It's given me goosebumps.'

'Let's hope the weather's not turning foul,' I add.

Geordie throws his cutlery down on the table. 'Oh, a pair of bloody comedians, eh? You two should have your own TV show.'

'Yes, come on boys,' Flaky starts. 'Leave it out. You're deliberately ruffling his feathers.'

'Right, that's it!' Geordie explodes. 'I shall eat my lunch in the confines of my tent, away from your childish banter.' He grabs his plate and marches off, albeit with some discomfort.

'What a peculiar gait,' Flaky notes.

'It's called a slow-motion goose-step,' Robbo sniggers.

*****

The raucous, cackling laughter of the children rudely brings my afternoon catnap to an end. They are singing some sort of nursery rhyme outside my campervan. I wearily lift my head, move the curtain back and stare at them. They're in a conga-line, swaying from side to side, as they kick one leg out to the right, then one leg out to the left, as they stumble forward, chanting a rhyme.

'Goose, goose, cock. Cock, cock, goose. Goose on the loose. Cock in the goose is no excuse, it is known as goose abuse. Goose on the cock will give you a shock, you will need to call the goose abuse doc. Goose on the loose goes cock, cock, cock!' They repeat it over and over as they shriek with laughter. It was worth being woken up for and brings a smile to my face. Unfortunately, the inventive rhyme is curtailed as the formidable figure of Jackie materialises.

'Children! Stop that at once! It's vulgar. I don't want to hear you using language like that again. Do I make myself clear?' she yells.

'Aw, mam! You always spoil our fun,' Wallace laments as the children disentangle themselves from each other. I step outside and join Flaky and Robbo who are sitting around the table.

'I'm telling you, it's absolutely fine. I've been nibbling on it all day,' Flaky says as Robbo sniffs at the cheese.

'It smells off, and it's very runny,' Robbo says as he turns his nose up.

'It's supposed to be runny. You eat it at room temperature, that way it brings out the flavours.'

'Hey, Will, come and smell Flaky's cheese? Tell me if it's off or not.' I sit down and stare at the cheese.

'No thanks,' I say.

'Come on, smell the cheese,' he insists.

'I'm not smelling the bloody cheese!' I pull a beer out of the cooler box and crack the top. 'I've just seen Jackie scolding the kids, but where are the others?'

'Gillian, Julie, and Fiona went for a walk along the beach. I assume Geordie and Jackie were having a snooze, until the children's impromptu singalong,' Flaky explains as he places a cheese and cracker into his mouth.

'It was very good,' I say.

'They were dead quiet for about an hour. I reckon they were working on it in the boys' tent,' Robbo adds.

'Here they come now,' I say as I nod towards three distant figures ambling up the field.

'Pass me a beer,' Robbo says as he lights a spliff.

'Aye, you can get me one too,' Geordie's voice booms out as he walks around the corner of the motorhome. 'Did you hear those bloody kids? I don't know where they get it from,' he says with a wry smile.

'You seem in a better mood. Has the swelling gone down?' I ask.

'Aye, a tad, but it's still bloody sore. Here, take a look,' he replies as he pulls at the waistband of his shorts.

'Bugger off! I don't want to look at your craning Cyclops,' I say, appalled at the very suggestion. He pulls up a camp chair and slumps into it as he glugs on his beer.

'Geordie, try this cheese. It's very good,' Flaky insists. Geordie looks disdainfully at the ever-diminishing gloopy mess.

'Nah. It looks like something the cat threw up. Plus, no disrespect to old Clarence, but I'm not sure he's the most hygienic person on the planet. I bet he made it from raw cow's milk. You need to be careful with soft cheese, you can get wisteria from it.'

'It's listeria, you imbecile and I'll have you know that raw milk is far better for you than pasteurised,' Flaky says with his annoying all-knowing manner. 'Humans drank raw cow's milk for thousands of years.'

'You're probably correct. That's why the average lifespan was about twelve years of age.'

'It has life-giving properties,' Flaky continues.

'It will have life-ending properties if you keep banging on about it,' Geordie replies.

'Suit yourself,' Flaky says as he finishes the last morsel.

'Robbo, roll me a spliff,' Geordie says as he finishes his beer in near record-breaking time and grabs another.

'I thought Jackie had curtailed that little avenue of relaxation a long time ago?'

'What the eye doesn't see the heart doesn't grieve over. Anyway, I'm my own man. I can do as I please and if she doesn't like it, she can lump it,' Geordie replies as he takes the joint and lighter then sparks up. 'Oh yes... that's better. Anyway, it's for medicinal purposes. I'm a man in pain... not that I like to talk about it. You know me, I'm not one to bring other people down by moaning about my ailments.'

'Hey, when was the last time one of you lot got your leg over?' Robbo quizzes, completely changing the subject. 'I haven't had it since we arrived,' he adds, glumly.

'I'm in the same boat,' I reply. 'It's pretty hard to do when you're in a motorhome with your child in there. Not that I haven't tried. I nearly got lucky this morning until Mary appeared on the scene.'

'We only arrived yesterday!' Flaky exclaims with astonishment. 'Are you telling me you can't forgo sex for seven days?' Me, Robbo, and Geordie exchange confused glances.

'No, of course not,' we all reply together.

'You're pathetic. All three of you are addicted to alcohol, smoking, and sex.'

'It's called the Holy Trinity,' Robbo says.

'And long may it continue,' Geordie adds.

'Have you no higher calling in life than satiating your cravings and desires?' We all stare at him blankly. 'There's not an ounce of spirituality in any of you. Do you ever wonder how you got here?'

'Straight down the M6 and onto the M5 after West Bromwich,' Robbo says.

Flaky shakes his head. 'It's pointless. I'd get more sense out of the children. One day you're going to leave this world and when you do, you'll regret the life you've lived.'

'Listen up, Mother Teresa, I'm having the time of my life and have no regrets about anything. I'm living the dream… we all are. You should be eternally grateful to us,' Geordie snaps, rising to the bait.

'Oh, and why's that?' Flaky asks. *Here we go.*

'You're hardly the greatest drummer in the world, are you? You've ridden on our coat-tails for most of your adult life. If it weren't for us, you'd be a pen-pushing bean-counter like that poor old sap, Twitchy. You'd have been shown the door a long time ago if it weren't for Billy Boy's misguided loyalty towards you. Me and Robbo would replace you in a flash.'

'Eh up, don't bring me into this. I'm minding my own business having a quiet smoke and a beer. I don't need the grief.' Flaky jumps to his feet.

'How dare you!'

'Boys, boys, boys,' I begin. 'These petty arguments belong in the recording studio, *not* on a campsite whilst we're on holiday. I'll say one last thing then let's drop the subject. Flaky, if you ever bothered to listen to our music, then you'd realise that is where our spiritual side lies… in the songs.'

'Well said, Bill.' Flaky resumes his seat, bearing a wistful, faraway expression on his face.

'I'm sorry,' he murmurs. 'I didn't realise you all felt that way about me.'

'Flaky,' I begin, 'stop being a dick. Of course, we don't feel that way about you. You're as much a part of this band as anyone. It wouldn't be the Shooting Tsars without you. It's the nature of being in a band together. The bickering, arguing and piss-taking gives us an edge. If we were lovey-dovey with each other all the time, our music would be shite. We're like brothers. We annoy the crap out of each other, but it doesn't mean we don't care. I thought you would have realised that after all these years.'

Flaky smiles. 'Yes, I know. As I said, I'm sorry.'

'I'm sorry too. Apology accepted. You sanctimonious, ferret-faced, old hen,' Geordie adds with a grin.

Flaky laughs. 'Fair enough.'

'How the hell did all this start?' Robbo drawls. 'One minute we were talking about the lack of sex, the next minute it's World War 3.'

'It serves you right,' Geordie says as he takes a long and lusty toke on his joint. He holds it in for a while then emits a massive plume of white smoke into the air.

'What serves me right?' Robbo says, confused.

'It serves you right for hiring a motorhome instead of camping. That's why I bought a second tent for the boys. You've got to think ahead. I'm not bragging, but I've already been well served in that department. Although, taking into consideration my current predicament, not that I like to talk about it, I'll be refraining from coitus tonight.'

I nearly spit my beer out. 'Coitus! I didn't realise you spoke Latin.'

'Geordie!' Jackie's voice echoes out. Geordie jumps out of his skin as he quickly hands the half-smoked joint to me.

'Here, take this,' he whispers.

'Sweet merciful crap!' she bellows. 'What the hell is Robbo smoking! Talk about "Puff the Magic Dragon". They'll be able to smell it in Bristol!'

'You know what he's like, love', Geordie replies as Jackie comes marching around the corner. 'I have tried to warn him about the consequences of the habit, but where there's no sense there's no feeling.' She eyes him suspiciously, then turns her attention to me.

'It's a long time since I saw you with a joint, Will?'

'I'm on holiday.'

'I thought cannabis didn't agree with you?' she persists, readjusting her attention back onto her husband, scanning him for the slightest sign of guilt.

'It was a minor disagreement. We've made up now.'

'Hmm... is that right? Because Geordie's been off the weed for... oh, how long would it be now, Geordie?'

'I couldn't tell you, my love. It was such a petty and insignificant part of my life, it's been eradicated from my memory.'

'Good. Make sure you keep it that way. You don't want to end up like Robbo.'

'What does that mean?' Robbo says, appearing hurt and confused at the same time.

'Nothing,' Jackie replies absentmindedly as she becomes distracted as the other women approach. Her demeanour automatically changes from a severe, matronly frown, to a smile, backed up with laughter lines. She trots out to greet them and begins laughing as she regales them with the tale of "Goose on the Loose." As they near, I can't help but admire them. Four beautiful women, not only in looks but also in spirit. *How did us four end up with such stunning women? Let's face facts—we're not the bonniest looking buggers doing the rounds. I wonder if they fell for our charm and wit? Nah! Don't talk daft. We have about as much charm as a shit sandwich. Maybe it was our brains? Ha! That's even more laughable. That only leaves one thing... they're all gold diggers. Yes, that's more plausible. Ah, well, I can live with that. Who said money can't buy you love?*

'Any plans for dinner?' Fiona asks no one in particular. 'We're all famished.'

'Yes, it's under control,' Flaky says. 'I'm going to do a Greek tuna salad with a chickpea and beetroot relish.'

'Bloody rabbit food,' Robbo complains.

'When was the last time you saw a rabbit eating tuna? If you don't like what's on the menu, maybe you'd like to provide a meal for eight adults and five children,' Flaky snaps at Robbo.

'If Robbo's cooking then I hope everyone's happy with baked beans on burnt toast,' Julie laughs.

'Righto, I'm going to prep,' Flaky says as he heads to his van. My eyes focus on Gillian. She's wearing an all-in-one, white swimsuit that is snug, to say the least. A long shirt is wrapped around her waist.

'I'm stiff for some reason,' she says as she raises her arms over her head and arches her back. I desperately try to avert my eyes, but my brain no longer has control over them. The man downstairs has taken control of the rudder.

'Who's for a glass of bubbly?' Jackie suggests. All the girls signal in the affirmative. A cooler, welcome breeze drifts across the campsite. Gillian unwraps the white shirt from around her waist and slips it on.

*****

Flaky did us proud. It was a tasty, light, and nutritious meal he served up and we are now all relaxing, sipping on wine.

'Flaky, I never thought I'd hear myself say this, but that bloody tuna salad was one of the best meals I've ever had,' Robbo proclaims.

'Thank you, Robbo. High praise indeed coming from someone who once tried to order a pot-noodle in a Michelin star restaurant.'

'Who's for another drop of red?' Geordie asks as he lifts the bottle from the table. Robbo and I push our glasses forwards. 'Flaky?'

'No thanks,' he replies.

'Come on, what's wrong with you? I know you like a wee drop now and then,' Geordie persists.

'The fact is… I'm feeling a little queasy,' Flaky replies.

'You're looking more than a little queasy,' Robbo comments. Indeed, he does. His cheeks are pallid, and beads of sweat are bleeding from his brow, despite the temperature dropping. As Geordie replenishes our glasses, Flaky staggers to his feet like a man who has recently been run over by a lawnmower.

'Why don't you go for a lie down?' I suggest.

'Yes, I think I will. Something's definitely happening down below,' he mumbles as he readjusts his spectacles and totters towards Gillian.

'You don't mean you're getting an erection?' Geordie chuckles.

'No, definitely not. It's my tummy. Something's not right.'

'I warned you,' Robbo says. 'That bloody Bell End Cheese was off!'

'Please don't mention the cheese,' Flaky replies, swallowing hard. 'Excuse me for interrupting, ladies.' The women stop their idle chit chat. 'Gillian, I'm going for a lie down. I'm feeling a little nauseous.'

'Oh, okay. Do you want me to get you anything?'

'No, thanks. I…' He rocks back and forth and from side to side. I fear he could pass out at any moment. His cheeks involuntarily puff out as he tries desperately to keep the contents of his stomach where they belong. He doesn't succeed. A geyser of vomit erupts from his mouth and splatters Gillian. I get a sudden flashback to the climactic scene of The Exorcist. Fiona, Jackie, and Julie react by launching themselves backwards and falling off their chairs. They hurriedly pick themselves up and stand well back as Flaky emits another fountain of vomit over his immobile wife. A few hushed seconds pass in morbid anticipation. Just when everyone thinks it's over, Flaky snaffles the trifecta, and ejects another stream directly over Gillian, who remains mute, incapacitated. She reminds me of one of those poor unfortunate souls from Pompeii. Forever entombed in a casket of lava and ash… except, on this occasion, it's half-digested tuna salad and Bell End Cheese.

'Shit the bed,' Geordie mumbles.

'I'm so sorry… I… oh, no. I need to get to the toilet.' Flaky turns and wobbles towards the motorhome.

'Looks like it's going to come out the other end. I warned him about that damn cheese,' Robbo whispers as Flaky disappears inside the van. A slow, high-pitched sobbing fills the air as Gillian's shoulders heave up and down. The other women spring into action.

'Julie, grab the hosepipe near our tent,' Jackie orders. 'Gillian, stay where you are.' Call it a hunch, but I'm pretty certain Gillian isn't planning to head down to the local nightclub anytime soon. 'We're going to hose you down, then get you into the shower. Try not to be upset.'

'Bit late for that,' Geordie murmurs. Julie returns with the hosepipe with a steady stream of water flowing from it.

'Gillian, throw your wine glass on the ground, stand up and take your shirt off,' Jackie commands. Gillian is now quietly sniffing in between sobs. She drops the glass on the ground, stands and pulls her shirt over her head and discards it. 'Give me the hosepipe, Julie. Okay, Gillian, this is going to feel cold. I'll rinse your arms off, then we'll do your hair.' As Julie passes her the hose, Jackie throws a look in our direction. 'Geordie, go help Flaky!'

'Like hell, I will! Robbo, go help Flaky.'

'Oh, no, not me. I used to dry retch when I occasionally changed Sally's nappy. Will, you go help him.'

'Don't talk wet! The last thing you want when you've got a raging case of Montezuma's revenge is for someone to be lurking in the background. It's a solo affair.'

'Aye. Fair point,' Geordie agrees. Gillian holds her arms out as water is squirted over her. Fiona and Julie use their hands to rinse her off.

'Okay, bend over and we'll do your hair.' Gillian bends double letting her long locks fall earthwards. She's doused in more water as Fiona and Julie push their fingers through her hair trying to dislodge all foreign matter. The sight is quite fascinating. After about thirty seconds, Jackie tells her to stand upright and lift her arms into the air. Drenched from top to toe, the poor girl is now shivering violently. Unfortunately, her tight, white swimsuit becomes completely transparent. It leaves nothing to the imagination. Again, Fiona and Julie rub their hands over her as they brush bits of vomit away. Much against my better nature, I find it one of the most erotic sights I've ever witnessed and become transfixed. With a massive burst of willpower, I finally avert my eyes and focus on the less attractive sight of Robbo and Geordie, who are both staring, slack-jawed, at the soft-porn scene.

'Ahem, come on lads,' I mumble. They break their gaze, and both sheepishly look away.

'Yep, quite right. Poor lass. She's like a sister to me,' Geordie says, guiltily.

'Yeah, me too,' Robbo adds.

'Although… technically… she isn't,' Geordie continues.

'That's true,' Robbo agrees, as we all once again focus our attention on proceedings.

'Christ,' I whisper, as Jackie glances over at us.

'And what are you three numbskulls gawping at? Have you got nothing better to do?' she barks at us.

'Not at this particular moment,' Robbo whispers. A painful wail from the motorhome distracts us.

'I thought I felt the ground shake,' Geordie grins.

'I think we have lift off,' Robbo chuckles. With ablutions complete, Fiona wraps a towel around Gillian's shoulders and escorts her towards the van.

'I'm freezing,' Gillian says with chattering teeth. Julie runs ahead.

'I'll get the shower going,' she shouts.

'And I'll make you a nice hot cup of tea for when you get out,' Jackie says as she heads towards her tent. We're left alone. I spark up a cigarette.

'What a show. Hey, Will, I've been meaning to ask you,' Robbo says.

'About?'

'It's Sally; she's been nagging me if she can have a sleepover with Mary in your van.'

I know his little game. 'Is that right. Funny you should mention it, but Mary has been nagging for a sleepover with Sally in *your* van.'

'Listen to you two randy buggers! You're like a pair of dogs on heat,' Geordie scoffs. 'I tell you what, as I'm temporarily incapacitated, I'll invite all the girls for a sleepover in the boys' tent. They'll need their sleeping bags and a pillow. That's the sort of man I am. Willing to help out to ensure my best mates fulfil their sexual urges.'

'Oh yes! Game on,' Robbo exclaims rubbing his hands together excitedly.

'I wouldn't get too optimistic, Robbo,' I say.

'And why's that?'

'Because if you hadn't noticed, Flaky staggered into your motorhome by mistake. That place will stink to high heaven. Hardly conducive to romantic liaisons of an adult nature.'

'I don't believe it!'

'Robbo,' Julie yells, 'change of sleeping arrangements for tonight. I'll be sleeping in Gillian's van, which means you'll be sleeping with Flaky.'

'What the!'

'You heard me. Someone needs to monitor him and make sure he doesn't take a turn for the worse.'

'Why can't Gillian monitor him? She is his wife,' Robbo pleads his case. He receives a glower that could stop a raging bull dead in its tracks.

'Don't you think she's gone through enough,' she hisses. 'And when you get in there, make sure you open all the windows.'

'Bloody charming,' Robbo grumbles.

'Look on the bright side,' Geordie sniggers.

'What bloody bright side?'

'At least Billy Boy may get his leg over.'

'My heart soars for him.'

8: The Arm-wrestle

The carousel grinds to a halt as I help the kids off their horses.

'That was fun,' Katrina says.

'No, it wasn't. It was bloody boring,' Wallace grizzles.

'Stop swearing all the time,' Sally says, pointing her finger at him.

'You can't tell me what to do. You're not my wife.'

'I'm going to tell your mum when we get home.'

'See if I care. Uncle Will, can we go on the dodgem cars again?'

'No, Wallace. We've been on them three times and I'm not sure my old bones will take another battering.'

'What's that big thing over there?' Mary asks.

'It's the helter-skelter,' I say.

'What does it do?'

'It doesn't really do anything. You grab a mat to sit on, climb the steps, and slide down to the bottom.'

'So, it's a slide?'

'Yes.'

'Why don't they call it a slide instead of an Alka-Seltzer?'

'Helter-skelter,' I correct. 'I don't know. I guess the words make it sound fast, which it is.'

'Is it fun?' Robert asks.

'Yes, it's fun. Do you want to go on it?'

'Is it safe?' Katrina asks. She's the most conservative of the children.

'Yes. It's safe.' I spot Geordie and Robbo heading our way, carrying a tray of coffees and a box of doughnuts.

'That wanker in the coffee van was bloody useless,' Geordie growls as he hands me a cup. 'Twenty bloody minutes queuing up. About as much use as tits on a bull.'

'Right kids, you can have a few turns on the helter-skelter then it's time for a break,' I say. All the kids bolt across the amusement park as we follow behind.

'How have they been?' Geordie asks.

'Pretty good. Although Wallace has taken to swearing a little too often.'

'Bloody little bugger. He gets it off Jackie. She's got a potty mouth on her.' Robbo and I exchange raised eyebrows with one another. 'I'll have a word with him.'

The operator of the helter-skelter is a dour chap who has a rather sharp manner with the children.

'How much is it?' I ask him.

'It's 50 pence per go or you can buy a book of 10 tickets for a fiver.'

'How does that work?'

'What do you mean?'

'Do you understand the concept of discounting? You buy one of something at full price, but if you buy ten you're sometimes offered a discount for buying in bulk.'

'I don't make the rules, pal. That's the way it is.'

I sigh. 'Okay, give me a book of ten,' I say as I hand over five quid. He stuffs the note into his leather satchel that rests on his ample pot belly. He turns to the children.

'Listen up, kids. You take a mat and climb the steps to the top. Only one person is allowed down at a time. The next person in line can't go on the slide until they see the first kid get off at the bottom. Do I make myself clear?' he barks at them. They all nod as though they've already done something wrong.

'You've certainly got a way with children,' I say.

'Kids are like dogs. They respect strength and straight talking.' I'm not entirely convinced dogs respect straight talking, but what do I know. The children all dutifully pick up a mat and race up the steps. 'Oi! Single-file and no running!' he yells. 'Little bleeders,' he mumbles under his breath.

'What do you do in the off-season?'

'I'm a children's entertainer.'

'Of course, you are.' Geordie and Robbo amble up. Geordie nods with pride at the children as they disappear around the first bend on the stairs.

'They're having a ball.'

'Yes, they are.' Sally and Katrina make their way back down looking worried.

'What's wrong?' I ask.

'It's Katrina,' Sally begins. 'She's scared.' Katrina stares at the ground, looking more embarrassed than frightened.

'What are you scared of?' Geordie asks as he kneels and gently lifts her chin up with his finger.

'It's really high,' she mutters. Geordie rubs her on the head.

'Not to worry. Your Uncle Billy will go up with you.'

'I'd love to, but I'm going to get the ice creams.' Geordie throws me a disapproving glance.

'Oh well, I'm sure your Uncle Robbo will hold your hand on the way up. Come on, Robbo, stop feeding your face for once and look lively.' Robbo devours the last of his doughnut as he stares up at the helter-skelter.

'Not on your nelly. I get a nosebleed going up the stairs at home. Why don't you take her?'

Geordie loses patience. 'Aye, okay. If you want a job doing, do it yourself. Come on Katrina, obviously, your Uncle Bill and Robbo are scaredy cats. We'll show them, eh,' Katrina smiles as she grabs Geordie's hand. The slide operator blocks him.

'Sorry, can't you see the sign,' he says. 'No adults allowed down the slide.'

Geordie glares at him. 'Out of my way, wee man. I'm not going down the bloody slide. I'm holding her hand until we get to the top.' The man reluctantly stands aside. As the three of them disappear from view, Wallace comes whizzing down the slide, squealing with delight. He immediately jumps to his feet, picks his mat up and races up the steps again. Robert arrives next followed by Mary then Sally. There's a slight delay until Wallace once again comes spiralling down.

'What's happened to Katrina?' I ask.

'Oh, she's still scared. My dad is trying to calm her down. Can I have another go?'

'Okay, I suppose so.' I buy another pack of ten tickets, drain the dregs of my coffee, and throw the cup into a bin. 'Come on, Robbo. You can give me a hand with the ice creams. Hey, where's Flaky?'

'He's gone to buy a postcard to send to his mum.'

'Do people still do that?'

'Apparently, some do.'

The children are sitting mute on a bench next to the slide. It's amazing how an ice cream cone can bring about silence. I gaze up at the boom lift of the fire engine as it reaches the top of the helter-skelter.

'How high do you think it is?' I ask Robbo.

'It must be over fifty feet, at least.'

'Hmm…' I spot Flaky mulling about in the distance and call him over. 'Did you get a postcard?'

'Yes; bought, written and posted.'

'How's the stomach, still feeling queasy?'

'A little. I've just eaten a cauliflower pie and had no repercussions, so I think I'm on the mend.' He peers at the children then looks around. 'Where's Geordie?' I raise my eyes heavenwards. He takes his glasses off, cleans them on his shirt, then stares up at the boom lift. 'No! Don't tell me the blockhead is being rescued from the helter-skelter?'

'You got it in one,' Robbo says stifling a yawn.

'Good grief! The man is a bloody liability. Wherever we go, whatever we do, Geordie always finds a way to stuff things up. He's a fully paid-up member of the Half-Wit Society. How did it happen?'

'He went up with Katrina as she was scared of the height. Then, for reasons best known to himself, he came back down via the slide. Katrina said he fell off the mat on the first bend and got stuck,' I explain.

'He is a big unit,' Robbo adds. The hydraulic whir of the boom lift cranks up again. As it slowly descends, I can hear Geordie and the lead firefighter exchange barbs.

'Don't you think we've got anything better to do than rescue adults from kiddie's rides?'

'Oh, I do apologise but it was on my bucket list to get wedged arse backwards on a bloody helter-skelter.'

'You should know better at your age. It's always the men, never women.'

'Chill out! It's not like you were doing anything else apart from playing poker and eating biscuits back at the station.'

'I'll have you know there's a lot of administrative work to be done when we're not on active duty.'

'Oh aye, you can spend hours on those porn sites.'

Flaky shakes his head. 'Why can't he ever admit he's in the wrong, take his medicine and get on with it? There's always truculent bickering.' I glance at the kids. Normally they'd be excited at watching the spectacle of a fire engine being used to extricate Geordie from a slide, but they appear blasé as they lick their ice creams.

'How come your dad always gets into trouble?' Mary asks Wallace. He contemplates the question for a moment.

'Hmm… my mam says he can't see the consequences of his actions.'

'What does that mean?' Sally inquires.

'I'm not sure, but I think it means he does things without thinking.'

'Uncle Geordie's funny,' Mary adds, with a giggle.

'It's not Uncle Geordie's fault,' Katrina says crossly. 'He was only trying to help me because I was scared to go down the slide by myself. He was being kind.'

'He was being stupid,' Robert giggles.

'Don't say that about your dad! It's rude,' pouts Katrina. It looks like Geordie has at least one fan. The bickering between Geordie and the firefighter continues unabated as the small crowd that had gathered for the free entertainment disperses.

'This is one of our busiest times of the year with traffic accidents and camping stoves going up,' the firefighter says as he opens the gate of the boom platform and steps out, followed by Geordie.

'Ah, stop your complaining man! You're still getting paid, aren't you? You've got to justify your wage packet, somehow. And may I remind you, hardworking taxpayers, like myself, pay your wages.'

'You'll be paying even more after this little escapade. This was a non-emergency call out which means I'm obliged to charge you for it.'

'You must be bloody joking!' Geordie yelps.

'I kid you not. I'll need to get your details and you'll receive a payment notice within thirty days.'

'Strike a light! How much is it going to cost me?'

'An hour of our time equates to about £320, depending on how many firefighters were called upon, plus administrative costs.'

'Bloody charming! Another example of capitalism gone mad. Making money from other people's misfortune. May I remind you it wasn't me who called you out in the first place; it was the bloody ride owner.'

'Geordie, wind your neck in,' I advise. The other firefighters troop back into the cab as the leading firefighter takes down Geordie's particulars. I wander over and eavesdrop.

'Aye, that's correct, 83 Main Road, Waddlington, Lincoln,' Geordie repeats, giving the firefighter Flaky's home address. Eventually, the kerfuffle is over. There's a quick blast from the fire truck's siren as it edges slowly away through the crowds.

'Right, who's for a refreshing ale at The Railway?' Geordie says, clapping his hands together, as though nothing has happened. 'It's got a nice beer garden so it will be perfect for the kids. We'll get them some crisps and lemonade.'

'I think they've eaten enough rubbish for one day,' starts Flaky. 'You heard what the girls said, not to get them sugared up.'

'Nonsense! Have you forgotten what it's like to be a child?'

'Hardly likely while ever I'm in your company,' Flaky moans.

*****

Geordie slaps his £20 note on the table.

'I'll take you on,' he states in a cocky manner. The two twins, Ginger and Nutmeg, eye him up suspiciously. They're stocky little buggers with biceps like Popeye. There's a small crowd gathered around the arm-wrestling table. The referee picks up the money and slides it into a leather wallet.

'Challenger,' the referee says looking at the twins. One twin nods and takes up his position.

'Do you know the rules?' the ref asks Geordie.

'Aye, I think so. Elbow on the elbow mat at all times. Free hand to grip the hand peg. The winner is the first one to pin his opponent's hand onto the touch pads.'

The referee nods. 'Good.'

'Who am I actually playing against?' Geordie asks.

'Your opponent is Nutmeg.'

'Doesn't say much, does he?'

'He lets his arm do the talking.'

'A talking arm, that's novel. He should join the circus.'

'Okay, take your grips.' Nutmeg dips his palm into a box of powder and rubs his hands together as Geordie places his right arm in the vertical position on the table. I spot Flaky exit the toilet and call him over.

'Of course, I knew he wouldn't be able to resist,' Flaky says as he stares disapprovingly at Geordie. 'I'm going to enjoy watching him lose. Geordie, these guys obviously make a living out of this game, do you really think you can beat them?'

'I do. Otherwise, I wouldn't have put my money down.'

'They're half your age, have biceps like cannonballs and are experienced.'

'Your point being?'

'You've just blown twenty quid,' Flaky chuckles.

'Don't you worry about me. Get the drinks in and quit your wittering.'

'Fine, have it your way,' Flaky replies as he heads towards the bar. Geordie and Nutmeg lock hands.

'Ready?' the ref asks. They both nod their agreement. 'Go!' Nutmeg goes straight in for the kill and almost pins Geordie's hand to the touch pad. They both stare intently at one another.

'You nearly had me there,' Geordie says, sporting a wide grin, whilst maintaining his hand an inch above the touch pad. The veins on Nutmeg's head bulge as he tries to end the match. Despite his best efforts, Geordie's arm is not going anywhere. Flaky returns with two pints of Guinness and places them on a shelf.

'I'm amazed the imbecile has lasted this long,' he states with mild surprise. As the minutes tick by, it appears we've entered a stalemate. Neither players' arm makes any progress. I lazily sup on my pint as Flaky disappears back to the bar. The crowd has grown in size. The locals are obviously not used to seeing their hero put to the test. A bead of sweat slides down Nutmeg's temple and onto his reddening cheeks. Geordie looks unperturbed as he throws me a glance.

'How's the Guinness?' he nonchalantly asks.

'Particularly good,' I say, taking a hefty quaff. Geordie licks his lips and flips his right arm up, then down with some force, pinning Nutmeg's hand to the touch pad. There are gasps from the throng. I hand Geordie his pint as the referee opens his wallet and peels off a slew of notes.

'Piece of piss,' Geordie says as he takes a few gulps of stout. 'Hmm… you were right, this is a bloody nice drop.' Nutmeg seems in pain as he bends his wrist back and forth whilst grimacing. He whispers to his brother, who throws Geordie a concerned glance. 'Right, I'll see if his numpty brother wants a go.' The referee hands Geordie his cash. 'Hey, big man,' he calls out to Ginger. 'How about double or quits… if you're up to it?' There's more discussion between the twins as Nutmeg points at Geordie's right arm. I think they've concluded that he's right-handed, and he'll be using his weaker left hand for the next battle. If they have… it's the wrong conclusion. Ginger smiles and nods at Geordie.

*****

I carry the tray of drinks into the beer garden, followed by Geordie.

'We better make this the last one and get back to the campsite. The girls will wonder where we are,' I say as I hand the drinks out.

'No, they won't. They'll be enjoying the peace,' Geordie replies.

'How did you go with the arm wrestling?' Robbo inquires. Geordie grins at him and pulls four hundred quid from his pocket. He flutters it back and forth in Robbo's face.

'Like taking candy from a baby.'

'Oh good, that means you can pay me back what you owe me.' Geordie hurriedly stuffs the notes back in his pocket.

'Don't worry about that now. Anyway, I like to have a little cash on me. I may even have a small wager on the gee-gees. Where's his Holiness?' he asks, referring to the absent Flaky.

'He's taken the kids down the street to buy a kite.'

'Has he been drinking?'

'Lemonade.'

'Good. He can drive back. We can get another two or three pints in. Bottoms up boys!' We clink our glasses together.

9: The Wager

We spent a pleasant morning on the beach with the children building sandcastles, searching rock-pools and paddling in the icy waters of the Bristol Channel. I'm now enjoying a relaxing lunch of cheese, thinly sliced ham, pickles, and hearty chunks of French bread. A lazy, relaxed hush has fallen over the camp. The kids have entered silent mode, always a good sign. It means they're tired due to the energetic morning. I'm pretty confident they'll find a quiet spot and read a book or maybe have a little snooze after they've finished their food. It means I'll get the afternoon to myself. I fancy reading a book or doing a crossword, with a chilled bottle of Pinot Gris by my side, followed by a power-nap. That's the thing with holidays; activity needs to be tempered with laziness. They're perfect companions.

A little later, and my predictions come to fruition. The children departed to the boys' tent about twenty minutes ago, and it's gone very quiet since. Fiona has a quick peek at them through the insect screen before she makes her way to the table where the rest of the women are sitting. She plonks down into a camp chair and picks up a book.

'Aw, that's sweet,' she gushes.

'What is?' I ask.

'Mary and Sally are lying down reading the same book and the boys and Katrina are fast asleep. It's so cute.' I rub my hands together in gratification. Robbo and Geordie finish drying the last of the lunchtime pots as Flaky pours the dishwashing water away.

'Are you boys ready for a nice glass of white and some chill out time?'

'Too bloody right,' Geordie moans. 'This camping malarky is hard work.'

'But enjoyable,' Jackie adds.

'Aye... I suppose it is. In its own way.' I pull out a bottle of wine from the cooler box and fill four glasses.

'At last, a bit of "me" time,' I say as I sip on my wine. The boys join us around the table. They sigh wearily as they take a glug from their glass.

Fiona puts her book down and gazes at us. 'You boys need to think about your fitness levels. It won't be long before you're on that desert island. You need to make sure you're super fit before you go.' *Give me strength! There she goes with a slight dig. I haven't stopped since I arrived. The first chance of relaxation and she has to bring up the bloody desert island nightmare and bang on about our fitness.*

'I'm super fit, already,' I reply. 'I do at least eight hours walking around the Dales each week.'

'Hmm... yes, that is true. But I'm not sure that makes you super fit,' my wife says as she smothers another cracker with soft blue cheese and washes it down with a large gulp of wine.

'Walking is *the* best form of exercise. As long as you go at a good pace and don't dawdle. It's easy on the body.'

'I'm with you, Fiona,' Jackie begins. 'There's far too much smoking, drinking, and eating fatty food if you want my opinion.'

'Well, you need to take a lesson out of our book and curb your excesses,' Geordie replies.

Jackie glares at him. 'I *was* talking about you four… or at least you three. Sorry, Flaky, I didn't mean to lump you in with the three wise monkeys.'

'No offence taken, Jackie. But I do agree with you. Their propensity for alcohol, cigarettes, drugs, and an unhealthy diet, is staggering. I'm surprised one, or all of them, haven't had a serious medical episode yet. Although, it's only a matter of time. No one is getting any younger. It won't be long before one of them falls foul to one of the big killers; heart-attack, stroke, lung-cancer, cardiovascular disease. Mark my words!'

'Oh, shut your cake-hole! You sanctimonious, holier-than-thou, wank goblin!' Geordie grizzles. 'I'm fitter than all of you! I'll see the lot of you into the grave by about ten years.'

'Ha!' Flaky scoffs. 'Dream on! I'm easily the fittest. I run two or three times a week and me and Gillian are in a local badminton team.'

'Badminton, indeed,' Geordie mocks, as he smashes his generous glass of wine back. 'Airy-fairy nonsense for the middle-class, PC brigade. It's hardly extreme sports.'

'And what exercise do you do?' Jackie scolds her husband.

'Excuse me!' he cries indignantly. 'I cycle.'

'Aye, down to the pub three times a week,' she says, bringing laughter from the other women.

Geordie looks hurt. 'That's not true… well, yes, it is true, but I don't only cycle to the pub.'

'Oh, really. Where else do you cycle to?' Jackie asks.

'Back home again,' the simpleton replies.

'I'll have you know I've been swimming every day for the last three weeks,' Robbo states, entering the fray.

'He has, I can vouch for that,' Julie confirms.

'I'm up at the crack of dawn every day and down to the local pool,' Robbo continues with pride.

'It's usually about 11 o'clock. That's what he calls the crack of dawn,' Julie informs us.

'And exactly how far do you swim?' Geordie asks with a degree of scepticism.

'Twenty-five lengths.'

'Is this in the kiddies pool?'

'You may mock Geordie, but let's face facts. I may not be the fittest in the band, but I'm fitter than you.'

'Codswallop. I'm by far the fittest. Fitness is not about what exercise you do. It's down to your genes, and I'm a natural born athlete. When I was at school...'

'Oh no! Not the school thing again! That's nearly twenty-five years ago,' I exclaim.

'You never lose it, Bill. I'd wager I am definitely the fittest here.'

'Let's prove it,' Flaky declares.

'I don't need to prove it, sunshine,' Geordie responds.

'No, of course you don't... you big wuss. I was going to suggest a race, but obviously, you're scared of losing.' Geordie cracks open a beer, necks it down in one, and slams the bottle onto the table.

'Scared of losing, am I? Wuss, am I? Okay, we'll have a race... the four of us!'

'When?' Flaky sneers.

'Tomorrow morning... 10:00 am.'

'Okay... you're on,' Flaky replies with glee. Sweet merciful crap! Where did this come from? All I wanted was a quiet afternoon filling in a crossword, sipping on wine, followed by a snooze. Now it looks like I'm an automatic starter for the fuckwit Olympics.

'How about a run along the coastal path and across the beach to Flexley? Then back along the main road to the campground,' Flaky suggests.

'You're on,' Geordie says, puffing his chest out. 'Are you two marshmallows up for it?' he says nodding at me and Robbo.

'Count me in,' Robbo agrees, much to my surprise. The last thing I want to do on my holiday is to go for a competitive run against these three clowns.

'Oh, I know girls,' begins Gillian, 'why don't we organise a sweepstake? £10 each. We'll put four names in the hat and the winner takes all.' The other three wholeheartedly agree with cries of laughter.

'Oh yes! That will be fun,' Fiona says. 'I hope I pull Flaky's name out.'

'Thank you very much for your vote of confidence, dearest!' I say, more than a little miffed at her betrayal. She looks contrite.

'Oh, I'm not saying you'll come last. But I'm not certain you'll come first.'

'Face facts, Bill, this is a two-horse race between me and Flaky. You and blubber boy, over there,' he says, nodding at Robbo, 'have no chance. You two can fight it out for third and fourth spot.'

'Oi, who are you calling blubber boy?'

'Okay,' I say, agitated enough by their self-preening and grandstanding, to make a rash decision, 'let's do it! Game on. I'll show you lot.' Flaky is beaming like he's won a free night in a brothel. 'First, we need to establish the rules to make sure there's no cheating.'

'Excuse me! But I'm a man of honour! There's no way I'd cheat,' Flaky objects.

'Pipe down, brass neck,' Geordie quips.

'It's not you that worries me. It's these two degenerates I'm concerned with,' I respond, pointing at Robbo and Geordie.

'I take exception to that,' Geordie argues.

'You can take whatever you want to it, but I want cast-iron rules in place so you two can't wangle your way out of the result. When I win this race, I don't want you two coming up with ridiculous excuses.'

'Agreed. What are the rules?' Robbo asks.

'The coastal route to Flexley, on foot, and back to the campsite along the main road. A staggered start by say... fifteen minutes. That way, no one really knows who's in the lead and there can be no conspiracies hatched. We also need some sort of proof that we all actually reached Flexley. No taking a shortcut up the beach and onto the main road, bypassing the town.' Everyone falls silent for a moment.

'Ooh! I know,' begins Julie. 'The visitor information centre on the promenade. You can all pop in there and pick up a town map. That will be your proof.'

'Great idea,' I say. 'Fiona, pick four blades of grass and we'll sort out our starting positions. The shortest blade sets off first, longest goes last. Does everyone agree?' The other three nod. Fiona is back within seconds with four strands of grass clasped in her fist. We all pull one out. 'Right, that's settled then. Geordie starts at 10:00 am, followed fifteen minutes later by Robbo, then by me at 10:30 am and lastly, Flaky at 10:45 am. You girls can be the adjudicators. Record our departure and finish times. We'll set up a table and a finish line, next to Geordie's tent.'

'How far do you think it is, there and back?' Robbo mumbles, realising the enormity of the task for the first time.

'I'd say it would be a good hour along the coastal path to Flexley. Coming back, it's a lot more winding and uphill. I reckon the return leg, along the road, would be a good two hours or more,' I say. Robbo sighs as he pulls out a reefer. Meanwhile, Flaky's grin grows ever bigger. Geordie's exuberant, cocky smile has evaporated.

'If the girls are having a sweepstake, how about you three put your money where your mouth is. What about a little wager?' Flaky suggests.

'I thought you were against gambling?' Geordie grumbles, realising what he's got himself into.

'I am. Organised gambling is the work of the devil. But a good-natured wager between friends is okay. I will bet £300 that I come first. Anyone care to take me up on it?'

'Winner takes all?' Robbo asks.

'Yes, Flaky takes all. Any takers?' His last arrogant statement has the rest of us bristling, and we all commit to the gamble. It was a masterful stroke of one-upmanship that I'd be quite proud of myself.

'By the way, when I collect my £900, I *will* donate it to charity.'

Geordie groans. 'Flaky, can you stand back a little,' he says.

'Why?'

'The reflection from your halo is blinding me!'

10: The Race

'Ready, set, go!' Jackie yells as she prods her phone to start the timer. Geordie sets off down the hill at a steady pace. Robbo is sitting at the side of me, rolling a joint.

'I'm not sure that's how Olympic athletes prepare before a big race,' I say.

'Good job it's not the Olympics then,' he replies as he places the joint behind his ear and picks up a grease filled bacon and egg roll.

'And the food of champions,' I comment.

'Fats,' he mumbles as a piece of egg slips onto his hairy, white thigh.

'Fats?'

'The body converts fat into energy before carbs. This bacon roll will be like an adrenalin shot to the arm.'

'Or the heart.'

'Where's Flaky? I've barely seen him this morning.'

'He's in the van meditating.'

'Dozy prick. He's taking this very seriously.'

'He is. I saw him earlier doing yoga, followed by callisthenics. He's been topping up with electrolytes all morning,' I explain as I take a gulp of coffee. 'Fancy your chances?'

'Nah, I've no chance of winning. But as long as I finish ahead of that moron, I'll be happy,' he says, nodding at the rapidly disappearing figure of Geordie.

'Ten minutes, Robbo, and you're up,' Jackie advises, peering at her timer. Robbo nods as he stuffs the last piece of roll into his mouth.

'Right, I better go take a dump,' he informs us as he creaks from his chair and lumbers towards his motorhome.

Julie sighs. 'He's such a charmer, isn't he?' she says.

'That's one word for it,' Jackie adds.

There are a few seconds to go before it's Robbo's turn.

'What's in the bumbag? ' I ask. 'A bottle of water?'

'Nah. Ciggies, lighter, and a bit of money.' Stupid question.

'What do you need money for?'

'I'm going to stop at the cafe on the front and get a couple of cinnamon doughnuts and a cup of coffee. It will give me the impetus to power on through the return leg and pass Lurch.'

I'm surprised at the speed Robbo takes off with. He resembles a bulldog that has been fired from a cannon as he flies down the hill. What I'm not surprised about is the ciggy that dangles from the edge of his mouth.

'I didn't expect that,' Fiona gasps. 'I thought he'd set off at a gentle jog.'

'Very impressive,' Gillian says.

'Hmm… don't be too impressed. He's probably got an appointment with his weed dealer,' Julie scoffs. 'Have you ever seen anyone running with a bloody cigarette in their mouth? He's like a throwback to the 1930s. I'm amazed he hasn't got a bottle of brown ale in one hand.'

Fifteen minutes have nearly elapsed as I make my way to the starting line.

'One minute to go, Will,' Jackie informs me.

'Fiona, can you massage my shoulders?' She dutifully obliges. 'Oh, yes, that feels good,' I say rolling my neck from side to side.

'What's wrong, a little nervous, are we?'

'Not at all. I just wanted a massage.'

'Ready, steady, go!' Jackie yells. I set off down the hill at a gentle jog until I reach the bottom. I scramble through the wire fence and take a right along the coastal path. The Sun is smiling high above and even with the gentle ocean breeze, I'm already feeling hot. As I come to the end of the track, I'm offered a panoramic view of the sand flats below. Flexley is nothing but a dot on the horizon. Its only distinguishable feature is the helter-skelter on the promenade. I experience a sudden twang of anxiety. The distance involved is far greater than I estimated. I can't see Geordie but I'm assuming the waddling blob in the distance, which appears to be walking, must be Robbo. I trot down the steps that lead from the cliff and jump the last two onto hard damp sand and set off again. There's nothing for it; I need to put my head down, get into the zone, and trundle on.

I pass people walking their dogs, lovers in arms, families picnicking on tartan blankets and children flying kites. This was a bloody silly idea! After well over an hour of jogging I near the Flexley promenade. The last two hundred feet are agonizing as the firm beach gives way to golden friable sands that swallow up my aching feet. My head and heart pound, my legs are like jelly and I'm parched. I stumble wearily up the concrete steps, stopping at the top to catch my breath. I turn and scan the horizon behind me. I spot Flaky in the distance and he's certainly not fifteen minutes away, maybe seven at the most—the smart-arse. The vision of him gives me a renewed sense of purpose, at least for a moment. I skip along the promenade, dart into the visitor information centre, grab a town map and stick it in my pocket. Instead of following the sea wall south and towards the main road out of town, I cross the street to the rows of shops on the other side. I need water. As I turn a corner, I stumble into a table outside a café.

'Eh, up, watch where you're bloody going!' a familiar voice cries out. It's Robbo. I lean on the back of his chair. He's sitting comfortably smoking a cigarette. 'Oh, it's you,' he says. 'Pull up a seat.' I flop down still unable to speak. The jingle of the door sounds as a waitress walks out.

'Your coffee and cinnamon doughnuts, sir,' she says placing them on the table.

'Thanks, love. Do you want anything?' he asks me.

'I'll have a long-black, large. Oh, and could you bring a jug of water and a couple of glasses?' I mumble between gasps.

'Of course, sir. It won't be long.' Robbo pushes his cig packet and lighter towards me.

'How long have you been here?' I ask as I spark up a ciggy. He checks his watch.

'Ten minutes.'

'That means I've closed the gap on you by five and I reckon Flaky has closed the gap on me by about ten.'

'That run across the beach was brutal. I got blisters within fifteen minutes. I daren't even look at my feet.' The waitress arrives with my order. I hurriedly knock back three glasses of water before starting on my coffee.

'Have you seen Geordie?' I ask.

'Not since the beach. Believe it or not, about halfway across I was actually closing the gap on him. Then he glanced over his shoulder and bolted.'

'You realise that Flaky or God forbid, Geordie, is going to win this.'

'I know. I'm not sure which one will be worse. Geordie's sarcastic gloating or Flaky's insufferable lectures about diet, smoking, and drinking too much.' We both stare at each other.

'Flaky,' we both moan in unison.

'Talk of the devil,' Robbo says. 'Here comes White Lightning right now.' I glance across the road to witness Flaky, panting hard, but still keeping up a steady pace as he pounds the pavement. 'Should we call him over?'

'No. He wouldn't come, anyway. He's a man on a mission.' He passes on with his head down, oblivious to our existence.

'Oh, no… just what we need. Don't look now, but Twitchy's heading our way.'

'Shit the bed! Keep your head down, he may not notice us.' We turn our heads slightly and stare at the ground.

'Morning chaps! Out for a run? Beautiful day for it.'

'Hi, Twitchy. What have you been up to?' I ask, instantly regretting it. Some people never learn.

'I was up at dawn and went down to Eagle Point. I spotted a pair of honey buzzards and two chicks. I estimated the male had a wingspan of at least 140 cm. Most magnificent! The honey buzzard is listed on schedule 1 of the wildlife and countryside act 1981. Only about 40 breeding pairs in the whole of the land. They winter in equatorial Africa and return to their breeding grounds at the beginning of our summer. They're a month or two early. Must be the warm spring we've had.' I wish I'd never asked. Not that it would have stopped him, anyway.

'Give me a gun, and I'll take all three of us out,' Robbo whispers. Twitchy waffles on for a further five minutes, as I lose the will to live.

'I'd like to stay longer, but I really must get myself over to Wadpole Ferns. There's a rumour circulating amongst the twitching fraternity that a pair of marsh harriers were spotted there last summer. I'm doubtful myself. It's not typically their sort of habitat, although it has been known that...'

'Well, don't let us stop you, Twitchy. Time is precious,' I interrupt.

'Yes, you're right. We can always catch up later tonight. I can show you my photos. Enjoy the rest of your day. Goodbye.' He ambles off.

'He could bore the tits off a nun,' Robbo grumbles.

'I've got nothing against a man having a hobby. But keep it to yourself. Don't thrust it onto other people.'

'I agree. He's a thruster. Nothing worse.'

'Hey, hang on, I've had a thought. Oi! Twitchy!' I yell.

'What the hell are you doing?' Robbo hisses, clearly alarmed. 'We've just got rid of him. Are you a masochist or what?' Twitchy stops and turns.

'Yes?' he says as he makes his way back to us.

'You said you were heading to Wadpole Ferns.'

'Yes.'

'You don't pass the campsite on your way by any chance?'

'Yes, I do. Why, would you like a lift?'

*****

Twitchy opens the door on his ancient VW Beetle and pulls the passenger seat forward.

'One of you hop in the back and the other can ride shotgun with me.' I quickly barge Robbo out of the way and jump in the back. There's a long coil of rope on the backseat and various cords and fasteners. 'Oh, throw all that gear onto the floor,' Twitchy says. I take up position behind the driver's seat, hoping that being out of sight will be out of mind. Robbo grimaces as he climbs into the front passenger seat.

'Bastard,' he murmurs. As we set off, I relax back and rest my eyes. Twitchy is already telling Robbo about the mating habits of sparrowhawks, to which Robbo occasionally mumbles, "I see", or "is that right, well I never."

To say Twitchy is a sedate driver is an understatement. He makes Flaky, who is the slowest driver I've ever had the misfortune to share a car with, look like a lead foot.

We crawl through the busy high-street until we're on the winding open road heading towards our destination. Twitchy's excited gibberish continues unabated as a wave of tiredness washes over me.

'Oh, another runner up ahead,' Twitchy announces. I open my eyes and spot Flaky on the opposite side of the road, about fifty-feet ahead. Robbo throws me a quick glance as we both slump down in our seats. 'I believe it's your friend, Flaky. Shall I stop and give him a lift?'

'Oh, no,' Robbo says, 'He wouldn't appreciate that. Once he's in the zone, he doesn't like anything to distract him.' As we pass him, I take a sneaky peek out of the back window. He looks completely twatted! His head sways from side to side and he's wearing a pained expression as he blows hard. I can't help but smile.

'Ha ha,' Robbo chuckles. 'Daft bugger!'

'Still no sign of Geordie, though.'

'No. I'd assumed Flaky would have chased him down by now. Maybe he's fitter than we gave him credit for.'

'No way! I can assure you his fitness bank account is way overdrawn. The only person in worse physical shape than him… is you.'

'Cheers, pal. I don't see you plodding the pavement.' I close my eyes again and begin to feel drowsy but within a few minutes, two loud blasts from a car horn make me start.

'Ridiculous,' Twitchy moans, squinting in the rearview mirror. 'Why is everyone in such a rush these days. He'll have to wait until I get around the corner.' The car rattles its way around the bend until we're on a straight stretch of road. He slows the car and pulls over to the left, slightly. The roar of a car engine intensifies as the vehicle behind begins to overtake. I peer out of the window at the passing taxicab. Geordie's colossal head is but a few feet away from me. He's staring dead ahead until he casually glances sideways. I grin, as our eyes lock onto each other for a split second before his gaze returns to the road ahead. He does a violent double-take and begins gesticulating wildly. I shrug and hold out my hands.

'I can't hear you,' I motion as we both wind our windows down, simultaneously.

'You dirty pair of cheating bastards! I knew you'd pull a stunt like this! You dogs! You cannae be trusted!' he shouts, pointing aggressively at me. As the taxi pulls away, I give him the finger.

We chug on for another ten minutes until we near the campsite.

'Just drop us up here on the left, opposite the entrance, and next to the irate Scotsman standing on the grass verge,' I direct Twitchy. He pulls the car up in front of Geordie, who has his arms crossed and is tapping his foot against the ground in an agitated fashion.

'Thanks for the lift, Twitchy,' I say, as we clamber out.

'Not a problem. I'll call around tonight and share a beer with you and tell you how I got on with the marsh harrier.'

'Great, I'll look forward to it,' I say as he drives off. 'Like a bleeding hole in the head.' I turn my attention to Geordie.

'Well, well, well! What a pair of conniving, double-crossing, scheming, turncoats. I can handle the deceit, after all these years I've become accustomed to it. But you two planned this in advance, didn't you?'

'No, we didn't. It was kismet,' Robbo says as he sticks a reefer in his mouth.

'Kismet, my sweet blue arse cheeks!'

'It's true. We bumped into each other at a café, then Twitchy turned up. As he was heading our way, we thought it too good an opportunity to miss out on.' I explain. 'Anyway, people in glass houses…'

'I had extenuating circumstances,' he replies looking sheepish.

'Oh, yeah, such as?' Robbo queries as he puffs on his smoke.

'I got a cramp.'

'That's no excuse. All runners experience cramps.'

'Not like the one I had. It was life-threatening.'

'I've never heard of anyone dying of cramp.'

'Anyway, you were first into Flexley and the last one out… where did you get to?' I ask.

'I called in at the Bald Badger for a quick pint of Speckled Hen, a Scotch egg, and to ring for a taxi,' Geordie replies, guiltily.

'Helped with the cramp, did it?' Robbo smirks.

'For your information—yes, it did. Not that it's any of your business.' I check my watch.

'What are we going to do now?' Robbo begins. 'If we all run into camp together, it's going to look mighty suspicious.'

'Hmm… you're right.' I pause for a moment to gather my thoughts. 'I know; how about Geordie trots in now, then fifteen minutes later you arrive, and after another fifteen minutes, I'll cross the finishing line.' They both eyeball me warily. 'Whoever wins, wins. There'll only be a few seconds between the three of us,' I explain. They don't look convinced.

'And how can we trust you? You're hardly a man of unblemished character. What's to stop you setting off before your allotted time?' Geordie questions, his eyes narrowing to slits.

'I give you my word,' I reply. There's a Mexican stand-off as we each glare suspiciously at one another for a few moments. All we're missing is Spaghetti Western backing music. 'Look, how about a truce? Whoever wins the £1200, we agree to split it three ways. We'll all be £100 up. There'll only be one loser—Flaky. What do you say?' Geordie smiles as Robbo nods. I hold my arm out. 'Hands on,' I say. Geordie places his big mitt over mine, and Robbo does likewise over Geordie's.

'Okay, deal,' they both say.

I spend the next twenty-five minutes dozing behind a stone wall, out of sight. It's pure bliss but ends way too soon as my watch lets out a rapid beeping alarm. I climb over the wall, cross the bitumen, and stand at the entrance to the campsite. Only ten seconds to go. I gaze down the long country road and can pick out a dot in the distance as it rounds a bend. *Christ! That must be Flaky. He's still a good hour away.* One more glance at my watch and I set off down the hill towards the corral of motorhomes to the sound of whoops and cheers from the women and children.

*****

I exit the shower, quickly dry and dress. As I step outside, I smile as I spot Flaky staggering down the hill. His limbs have lost all coordination. He looks like a man who has been lost in the Sahara Desert for a fortnight and has suddenly spotted an oasis. If I was a good man, which I'm not, I'd almost feel sorry for him.

'And last but not least,' I announce. The women all turn around and gaze at him.

'I really can't believe he's last,' Gillian says looking worried. 'He doesn't appear too good. I hope he's all right.'

'Christ,' Robbo murmurs. 'He's like a wino who's just dropped a dozen acid tabs. So, who's the winner?'

'I've told you; we're not announcing the results until Flaky has passed the finishing line,' Jackie responds. As Flaky nears, he spots me and Robbo. I wish I had a camera to record his expression. It's a cross between astonishment, bewilderment, confusion, and horror.

'Look at that mush,' Robbo chuckles. 'Pure gold.' Flaky passes the finishing line and collapses in a sweaty, panting heap on the grass. Gillian rushes to his side with a bottle of water, but he's too exhausted to take it.

'How… who… it can't be,' he stammers and gasps. Geordie exits his tent, drying his hair with a towel as he walks over to us.

'Hey, Jackie, have you seen the sunscreen?'

'Aye, it's in the portable shelves hanging in the bedroom.' Geordie stares down at the gasping, wheezing mess on the ground.

'Ah, the wanderer returns. Nice of you to join us, Flaky. What are you doing down there? Out of puff?' he says nonchalantly as he heads back to his tent. Flaky sits up.

'No, it's not possible. Proof, proof, where's their proof?' Fiona holds out three leaflets picked up from the information centre.

'Sorry, Flaky, but here's your proof.' Geordie returns and rubs sunscreen into his face.

'Have you announced the winners yet?' he asks.

'Hang on, I'm working out Flaky's time,' Jackie replies. Flaky drags himself onto a camp chair as Gillian passes him the water. He necks it down in one go. 'Ahem, here are the results in reverse order. In fourth place with a time of 4 hours, 12 minutes and 22 seconds is Flaky. A big round of applause, please, everyone.' Feverish clapping erupts amongst the women.

'I don't think coming last warrants any applause,' Geordie grumbles. 'We shouldnae be rewarding mediocrity.' He receives a vicious glare from his wife. Flaky looks like he could have a seizure at any moment. Jacki continues.

'In third place with a time of 3 hours, 4 minutes, and 35 seconds, is Will. In second spot is Geordie with a time of 3 hours, 4 minutes, and 30 seconds. Which means…'

'Hang on a minute, what about some bloody applause for me and Bill?'

'Shut up, you big lummox, you're ruining the moment. This means the winner of today's race is none other than Robbo, with a time of 3 hours 4 minutes and 26 seconds.' There's an eruption of cheers and backslapping from all, apart from Flaky who is still struggling for breath.

'If I hadn't stopped to tie my shoelace, I'd have had that in the bag,' Geordie reflects.

'There has to be some mistake. They must have cheated. There's no way they all beat me by more than an hour. I was only five to ten minutes behind Will, crossing the beach.'

'It's all about pacing, Flaky,' Geordie begins. 'All elite athletes do it. I think where you slipped up was going too hard, too early, probably trying to impress the ladies. I took it nice and easy across the sand, knowing how that terrain can sap your strength. It's like changing gears in a car. Start in first and move slowly through them until you're cruising in fifth for the last few miles.'

'Couldn't agree more,' Robbo says as he puffs cigarette smoke into the air. 'I hit the zone early, after that it was simply a matter of harnessing the zen.'

'But, but... it doesn't make sense. I'm the fittest out of all of you. And to lose by an hour defies the laws of physics.'

'If there's one thing I cannae stand, it's a poor loser. Me and Bill didn't win either, but do you hear us whining and griping about the result? No, of course you bloody don't! We take it on the chin, like men. You should take this result as a wake-up call. You overestimated your abilities and underestimated ours. Telltale signs of a narcissistic megalomaniac. Hitler and Mussolini both suffered from it and look what happened to them. You need to take a long hard look at yourself in the mirror.'

'I think every one of you needs to be congratulated,' Fiona adds. 'You really surprised us all. Haven't they girls?' she adds turning to her friends.

'Oh, aye,' Jackie replies a little doubtfully. 'They all did magnificently. Especially for three of them to be ahead by over an hour and barely sweating as they reached the finishing line.'

'That's what happens when you're finely tuned and in peak physical condition, my love. And may I say, I find your implied scepticism of the result hurtful and frankly, quite offensive,' Geordie states proudly and defiantly. Unfortunately, the big klutz doesn't know when to keep his gob shut and carries on. 'Unless you have hard facts or evidence to back up your scurrilous accusations, then I request you withdraw them at once.' Jackie pouts as she eyeballs her husband.

'I never actually accused you of anything,' she replies.

'You implied it,' Geordie says.

'And you overreacted. Possibly, the sign of someone trying to hide something.'

'I'm going for a lie down,' says Flaky. 'I'm completely exhausted.'

'And yet, look at these three,' Jackie says as she holds her arm out to me, Robbo, and Geordie. 'As fresh as daisies.'

'That's because we've had an hour to recuperate and the recovery time for elite athletes is far less than it is for your average loser.' She moves towards her husband.

'Can you look me in the eye and tell me you completed that race with no shortcuts?' Geordie gulps hard then laughs nervously.

'Aye, I can. Cross my heart and hope to die. We followed the route as stipulated in the rules. No shortcuts.'

'Hmm… if I find out you've lied to me, I'll hang your balls up as a trophy,' she whispers before wandering off followed by the other women.

'That's a bit of a whopper, Geordie,' I remark.

'Not at all,' he replies, full of bravado. 'If I remember the rules correctly, and I do, you said the outward leg was along the coastal route to Flexley—on foot, did you not?'

'Yes, that's right,' I say.

'Which we all dutifully abided by. And you also stated the return leg back to the campsite was by following the main road—did you not?'

'Yes, but…'

'You mentioned nothing about it being on foot.'

I scratch at my chin. 'Well, no, I never actually stated by foot, but the implication was…'

'Ah, ah, ah. Never mind what the implication was. Did you categorically state the return journey had to be on foot?'

'No.'

'I rest my case, your honour. We all completed the race according to the rules.'

'That's very true,' Robbo chirps in. 'We should commend ourselves on our initiative.'

'Correct! Righto, who's for a cleansing ale?'

11: The Charter

The boat ploughs on through calm waters. Flexley-on-Sea long since disappeared from view. When we set off, the Sun was yawning as it began another lazy day. Clarence had told us the fishing charter only ventured out a mile or two off the coast. After two hours powering west, breathing in petrol fumes, I'm guessing we are way further out than a couple of miles.

We're all gathered at the back of the boat sitting on damp benches. Bubbles, the skipper, has barely said a word to us since our first introduction at Flexley.

'Strike a light,' Robbo moans. 'I thought this was going to be a jolly little jaunt a few miles offshore. Cast a line in, chillax, and go with the flow. If we keep going any longer, we'll be able to pull in at Lisbon for a plate of sardines and a glass of chilled port.'

'I agree. It's not much fun,' Flaky whines, looking a little green around the gills.

'I didnae pay £60 to go on a bloody aquatic magical mystery tour,' Geordie says, adding his tuppence worth.

'You didn't actually pay anything... I did,' I reply.

He disregards my comment. 'Bill, have a word with Bubbles... see what's going on.'

'He's right, Will. This was all your idea,' Robbo confirms.

'Excuse me, but you were with me in Clarence's barn. You were as keen as I was. Why don't you go quiz Bubbles?' He pulls out a joint, and with some difficulty due to the breeze, sparks up. The lad has tenacity.

'I was humouring you. I was never that keen on a bloody fishing trip, which meant getting out of bed at 5:30 am. But you looked like a kid on Christmas morning. That cute little excited smile of yours melted my heart,' he chuckles. Flaky and Geordie grin.

'Fine! As usual, leave it to Charlie Chore to do the dirty work. You three ballbags stay where you are and I'll find out what's going on,' I snap.

'Good man,' Geordie says. I stagger and sway my way to the cockpit and push open the door. Bubbles has his back to me, as he leisurely swings the helm back and forth.

'Bubbles,' I call out.

'Huh,' is his only response. A rollie sticks out from the side of his mouth.

'The boys and I were wondering how much longer to go?' I say, staring at the back of his creased neck and shock of grey curly locks.

'Not much longer,' he replies in his somnambulistic, west country accent.

'That's sort of subjective, you know, a little abstruse.'

'I don't go in for those fancy words.'

'What do you mean when you say, "not much longer"? Does that mean ten minutes, an hour, two weeks, a decade?'

'Like I said… not much longer. You want to catch some fish, don't you?'

'The thought had crossed my mind, you know, paying for a fishing charter and all.'

'I've been on the water since I was a fourteen-year-old.'

'Hell! That's a long time to be at sea.' He ignores my comment.

'That's over forty years—man and boy. I'm going where the fish are.' I glance out of the window and can see the vague outline of land on the horizon.

'Christ! Is that France or Spain?'

'It's Cornwall. Probably St. Ives.'

'Are you telling me there are no fish between here and Flexley? What do they do at Easter? Pack their bags and holiday at the Cayman Islands?'

'Not long now,' he replies without emotion. I may as well be talking to a sprig of asparagus. I shut the door behind me and head back to my mob.

'What did he say?' Flaky inquires.

'We got talking about quantum physics and the meaning of life. Interesting chap. I could have spent all day chatting away. But the upshot is, there's not much longer to go.'

'What does that mean? Robbo asks. 'It's a bit vague.'

'As someone famous once said, "time is a concept invented by man." Just go with the flow.'

'Thank you, Socrates!' Geordie scoffs. 'And as another famous person once said, "we are here but three score years and ten." I didn't come on holiday to do a day trip into the North Atlantic. You lot may enjoy sitting around on your brains, but I, for one, don't,' he grumbles. 'Send a boy to do a man's job. Step aside, I'll get some sense out of Bubble Boy.' As he stands up, the boat's engine dies away until the only sound is the slosh of water against the hull.

'X marks the spot,' Robbo comments. Bubbles emerges from the bridge with a pair of binoculars in his hands.

'Is this it?' I ask. 'Can we get our lines in now?' He appears confused as if I've asked him when was the last time he ate a pickled onion.

'What? Oh, yes. This is the spot. Rods are up there,' he says, pointing at an array of fishing rods sticking out of rod holders. 'The bait is in the cooler box, next to you. The rods are hooked up. You'll need to attach a sinker onto the bottom swivel. Sinkers are in the tackle box.' The other three whirl into action, as I carefully assess my options.

Where's the best spot to stand so I'm out of harm's way of Geordie? Hmm... standing directly opposite him is fraught with danger. Standing next to him may work until he reels in his line. My safest option is diagonally opposite. It's not perfect, but it's the best of a bad bunch.

Geordie has already attached a sinker, the size of a small dumbbell, to his line and is eagerly attaching bait to three hooks. He totters to the back of the boat on the starboard side. I glance at Robbo and Flaky, who appear to be nervously going through the same checklist I went through, a moment ago. They're eyeing up the best vantage point on the deck to avoid injury. I'm not hanging about. I quickly bait my line, grab a small sinker, and take up my position on the port side nearest the bridge. Flaky decides that standing next to Geordie is his safest choice, which leaves poor old Robbo with the worst possible scenario—opposite Geordie.

'Stand back!' Geordie yells as he flicks his rod to the side. He immediately clonks Flaky on the noggin with the lead weight.

'You bloody, blithering idiot!' he screams as he rubs at his forehead. 'Be bloody careful!' *That didn't take long… it must have broken some sort of record.*

'Hey, Nobby-No-Mates, I was here first. Your problem is, you're spatially unaware. You're in my personal space. It's a dangerous habit of yours. Now stop your blabbing and get out of my way.' Flaky moves aside as Geordie swings the rod further back into the boat.

'Christ, Geordie, why don't you just drop your line over the side?' I suggest.

'Don't tell your grandmother how to suck eggs. You forget I grew up in a fishing village. You need to cast away from the boat. Fish aren't stupid, you know. They see the hull as a giant predator.' He heaves the rod back over his shoulder and catapults the line, sinker, and baited hooks into the air. There's a whistling sound followed by an almighty bang as the cannonball sinker clanks into the side of the boat. The dickhead has forgotten to uncock the bail arm on his reel.

'Nice start,' Robbo chuckles. Bubbles pulls his binoculars away from his eyes and throws a disparaging glance in our direction.

'Bloody out-of-towners,' he grumbles. Geordie is unperturbed by his aborted cast.

'Stand back!' he yells again. This time Flaky ducks for cover as the rod swings around once more.

'He's a menace to life and limb,' Flaky curses, jumping out of the way. 'I knew this was a bad idea.' This time he launches the line high into the air. It seems to fly on forever until a small splash in the distance signals its return to earth... or sea. The rest of us quietly drop our lines over the edge of the boat.

'Hey, Geordie, remember the last time we went fishing? We were with Chas on that Greek island,' I say.

'Aye, how could I forget. It's etched into my psyche. I still wake up with palpitations.'

'Is this the story of when the dolphin saved your life?' Robbo sniggers.

'That's right. If it hadn't been for that dolphin, I wouldnae be standing on this boat.'

'And I always liked dolphins... until now,' Flaky says, wistfully. Geordie ignores him and continues.

'Super intelligent creatures—dolphins.'

'Yes, I agree,' I say. 'Especially the one that saved your life. Apparently, it could speak six languages, had a master's degree in biochemistry and could rewire a house.'

'Oh, that's right... you can mock, Billy Boy, but us humans aren't as smart as we think we are.'

'At least some of us aren't,' Flaky murmurs. I place my rod in the rod holder and spark up a cigarette. I peer over at Bubbles, who seems decidedly disinterested in his paying customers and overly interested in something out at sea.

'Any nibbles?' Geordie asks. The man has zero patience. His line has been in the water for less than a minute.

'Give it time,' I reply.

There is something peaceful about standing on the deck of a small boat as it gently rocks back and forth, accompanied by the comforting slap of water.

'We're on!' Geordie cries out.

'Don't talk stupid. You've barely wet your line,' Flaky says with incredulity.

'I'm telling you; I'm getting bites. Another few nibbles and I'll strike.' We all stare at him. Sure enough, a few seconds pass and he jerks the rod upwards with unnecessary force and violence. The rod bends double, whether it's due to hooked fish or the bowling ball he has attached to the end, I'm not sure. He reels in at lightning speed. As the hooks lift out of the water, I'm as surprised as anyone to see three wriggling fish attached to them.

'Look at those little beauties!' Geordie exclaims with glee. 'Mackerel for lunch, boys.'

'I don't believe it,' Robbo says as he puffs on a spliff.

'Beginner's luck,' I say.

'There's no luck involved,' Geordie begins. 'Saltwater courses through my veins. It's all about technique and reading your environment.'

'It's all about bullshit,' Flaky responds as the fish are dumped on the deck.

'Flaky, grab that cosh and give them a bop on the head, then unhook them and throw them into the cooler box,' Geordie orders. Flaky appears horrified.

'No way! You do it! You bloody caught them.'

'I'm holding the rod, you big Jesse. Okay, Robbo, I'll let you do the honours.'

'I'll take a pass, but thanks for the offer.'

'What's wrong with you two? Have you never killed a fish before? Bill, help me out here. Put the wee creatures out of their misery.' Charming! I quickly unhook each fish, give it a swift crack to the head with the wooden cosh and toss them into the cooler box. 'While you're there, can you re-bait my hooks? Good man.'

'Anything else? A foot massage maybe, a shoulder rub, a quick one off the wrist?'

'No, the bait will do. Make sure you hook it on properly. There's a technique to it. It's the first mistake amateurs make, not attaching their bait correctly.'

'Don't worry about Will, he's a master baiter,' Robbo giggles as he turns his attention to his own rod, which is twitching erratically. 'Here we go, my turn.' In his rush to get his line back in the water, Geordie snags a hook on Flaky's jumper. As the ensuing argument and bickering escalates, I notice my rod sharply bend and release.

For the next forty minutes, we all catch a plethora of fish, mostly mackerel. Some are undersized and released, but there are enough keepers to feed everyone for lunch. The feeding frenzy eases, and the thrill of the catch slowly ebbs. A distant, but high-powered, engine distracts me. I nudge Robbo in the ribs and nod towards Bubbles. Robbo raises an eyebrow.

'What's his game?' he whispers.

'Not sure, but it looks like there's a speedboat heading our way. It's all very odd.' As the speedboat approaches, it slows to a more leisurely pace. Bubbles advances towards the bow and out of sight. Muted voices are carried on the breeze. Bubbles reappears followed by two men who carry small backpacks, are wearing hoodies and have their heads down, obscuring their faces. They are quickly ushered into the bridge and disappear from view. I assume they've descended into the cabin. The throaty growl of the engine starts up, accompanied by the clank and rattle of the anchor chain. Bubbles sticks his head outside.

'Okay, boys. Lines in. We're heading back.'

'You've got to be joking!' I say. 'We haven't even had an hour's fishing.'

'Sorry. Nothing I can do about that. There's a storm brewing and we need to get back to the safety of the harbour.' He shuts the door behind him. We all peer into the clear blue skies. There are a few streaky wisps of cloud high in the atmosphere, but apart from that... conditions look perfect.

'Illegal immigrants,' Robbo mumbles as he reluctantly reels his line in.

'Hmm... maybe,' I reply, puzzled, and annoyed by proceedings.

12: The Request

It's early afternoon and we've just finished a glorious lunch of gently fried mackerel fillets, seasoned well, and drizzled in fresh lemon juice and a splash of olive oil. A crusty French baguette, slathered with butter, is a simple but delicious accompaniment. Bubbles, for all his surliness and lack of social skills, did teach us how to fillet fish once we were safely back in harbour.

'That was delicious,' Gillian says. 'So fresh and tasty.'

'Straight from the sea and into the pan,' Geordie says as he collects everyone's plates and cutlery.

'I'll give you a hand washing up,' I offer. Robbo is relaxing in a camp chair, shades on, head back.

'I'm knackered. That early morning start and sea air has done me in.'

Geordie shakes his head in contempt. 'Aye, you sit there with your feet up and let me and Bill do the washing up. Don't worry about us.'

'Cheers, I won't.' A hush hovers over the campsite. The children are busily engaged in arts and crafts. The women are relaxing in their chairs.

'What's on for the rest of the day?' Flaky inquires.

'I want to chill out this afternoon,' I begin. 'It's been full-on since we arrived.' There's a chorus of agreement from everyone. I rinse a plate off and hand it to Geordie, who picks up a tea-towel.

'A nice quiet one, eh, Bill?' he whispers. 'A few beers, a snooze in the chair and maybe tonight we could all go out for a meal.'

'Sounds perfect.'

'Hello, fellow campers!' Twitchy's disembodied voice calls out.

'Oh, no! Bugger me backwards.' I groan.

'Will!' Fiona hisses at me, as Twitchy comes around the corner.

'I hope I'm not interrupting,' he says with a bright smile and eager eyes. Actually, yes, you are interrupting but that's not going to stop you, is it? It never does with people like you.

'No, not at all,' Fiona replies standing up to invite him into our cosy domestic setting. 'Pull up a chair. Can I get you a drink? A beer or a glass of wine?'

'That's it, we'll never get rid of him now,' Geordie murmurs to me.

'He might refuse,' I say more in hope than belief.

'That would be smashing. A dry white would be nice. Thank you!' Robbo lifts his shades and throws me and Geordie a cheesed off glance.

'I thought I'd come and give you an update on my avian adventures.'

'Strewth,' Geordie mutters.

'I have a whole heap of photos to show you. Some very rare specimens indeed.'

'Oh, that's a pity,' I begin. 'I'd love to stop and take a look, but unfortunately, I need to check the oil and water levels on the motorhomes. But I know Robbo and Flaky would be delighted to peruse your photos. Robbo was only saying, this morning, that he was wondering when you were going to pop over to show him your bird snaps. Isn't that right, Robbo?'

'Eh? Oh, yes… that's right,' he says through gritted teeth as he glares at me.

'Come on, Bill, I'll give you a hand with the motorhome. Best check the tyre pressures as well. You cannae be too careful when it comes to motor vehicle maintenance.'

'Robbo, Flaky, pull up your chairs! I have some amazing news. You will not believe what I spotted this morning?' Twitchy begins, looking like he's fit to burst.

'A dodo,' Robbo begrudgingly replies as he picks his chair up and dawdles towards Twitchy.

'Ha ha! No, wait for it… only the rarest breeding garden bird in the UK!'

'Really. I'll go to the foot of our stairs.' Geordie and I make a rapid exit as Twitchy reveals all.

'It's the black red… red… red…' Twitchy stammers.

'Redbreast?' Robbo cries in anguish

'No. The red… red… red…'

'Redwing?' Flaky says in a peculiar high-pitched tone.

'No. The black red... red... r... r... redstart!' Geordie and I disappear behind a motorhome, pull a couple of beers from the cooler, and wander off to the far edge of the field.

*****

After thirty relaxing minutes, we return to "Slash Your Wrists Valley". Twitchy is still in full throttle. Only Robbo, Flaky and Gillian remain.

'Where are the others?' I ask.

'Oh, they all had migraines and went for a lie down,' Gillian replies. I busy myself in the camp kitchen, rearranging things that don't need rearranging. Geordie sidles up to me.

'Christ,' he murmurs, 'I think Flaky and Robbo may need to be put on suicide watch after this.' I glance over at them. Flaky is sporting a pained expression, much akin to a man who has suffered a weeklong bout of constipation. As for Robbo, I think he may have passed on. They do say that when you've given up the will to live, death shortly follows. Gillian, however, seems genuinely interested in Twitchy's longwinded, tedious tales of feathered activity.

'Do you do this for a living?' she asks him.

'Oh, no!' he chuckles. 'I only wish I did.'

'What's your profession if you don't mind me asking?'

'Court jester,' Geordie murmurs as he helps me move things from one place to another then back again.

'I'm an accountant.'

Gillian's eyes light up. 'Really, oh, I must pick your brains. I'm the bookkeeper for the band.'

'The band?'

'Yes, The Shooting Tsars… Flaky, Robbo, Will, and Geordie. You must have heard of them?' Twitchy's puzzled frown furnishes everyone with the answer.

'Erm… the name rings a bell but…'

Gillian interrupts. 'I wonder if you could enlighten me on the upcoming VAT changes that apply to small business?'

'I never thought I'd live to see the day when I was glad for someone to talk about VAT,' I mumble. Twitchy appears a little taken aback by the change of topic as Flaky and Robbo quickly head towards me and Geordie… probably to help in needlessly shifting things around.

'Hell's bells,' Flaky whispers. 'That was unrelenting.'

'I need a beer and a jab in the eyeball with heroin,' Robbo laments. Twitchy has fallen silent as Gillian, undeterred by his lack of response, continues.

'Specifically, it's about the EORI, or Economic Operator Registration and Identification number. We do a lot of online sales with member states of the European Union. And although I've tried to get my head around the forthcoming rule changes, I find them rather ambiguous.' Twitchy hurriedly packs his camera away, slugs his wine back and stands up.

'I'm sorry, but that's not my area of expertise,' he says, glancing at his watch.

'But if you're an accountant, surely you're up to speed with the changes?' Gillian asks, clearly puzzled.

'Heavens is that the time,' he says glancing at his watch. 'I really must get going. I've taken up enough of your schedule and I have a rendezvous with some fellow twitchers.'

'We need to put that one in the memory bank,' Geordie remarks.

'What?'

'How to get shut of him… ask him a VAT question.' A few minutes after Twitchy's departure, the rest of the women miraculously materialise.

'Migraines all gone now, girls?' Geordie sniggers. They all quickly refill their wine glasses and take hearty slugs.

'My God! That was excruciating,' Jackie moans.

'The poor man. He has a terrible stammer. But good grief, he is mind-numbingly dull,' Julie adds. 'Robbo, roll me a joint.'

'Just as soon as I've rolled one for myself. Rest assured, I'm more desperate than you.'

'I found him quite interesting,' Gillian giggles.

'You need your bumps feeling, girl,' Jackie says. The meshing of gears and a noisy diesel engine distract me. I glance up at the entrance to the campground. A knackered old open-top truck rattles down the hill towards us.

'I wonder who this could be?' Flaky says. As the truck nears, I let out a deep sigh.

'Great,' I moan. 'Farmer Clarence Longdon. He sure likes to pop by. What is this place… a bloody drop-in centre for misfits?' The truck pulls up and Clarence jumps out. He walks straight over to the women.

'Ladies,' he says as he doffs his hat, that is a definite health and safety issue.

'Clarence,' they all say with barely disguised disgust.

'Nice day for it,' he says, cryptically.

'I need to check if I turned the gas off in the van,' says Fiona as she hurriedly departs.

'I'll come with you,' Jackie adds.

'And I've got some washing that needs hanging out,' Julie begins. 'You couldn't lend me a hand, could you?' she says, turning to Gillian. A ladies' man, indeed. Within seconds of his arrival, Clarence has dispersed the opposite sex in double-quick time. His eyes follow them until they're out of view.

'What's happening, Clarence?' Geordie asks. Clarence's lascivious smirk drops from his face, replaced by a deep frown.

'I'm in a spot of bother and I was wondering if you boys would be willing to help a poor, old farmer out?' Geordie pats the old lech on the shoulder and smiles at him.

'Of course. Whatever we can do to help, we will. Isn't that right, boys?' A few tumbleweeds roll past accompanied by the sound of crickets. 'Now, what's the problem?'

'I need to move my hale bales from my top barn to my bottom barn. Normally my farmhands would do it, but they've phoned in sick. One's suffering from a sprained wrist, the other from a hairline fracture to his forearm. I've told them about the bloody arm wrestling before, but they don't listen. It had to happen eventually. To make matters worse, my forklift has broken down and the mechanic can't get to it until later on today. So, I was wondering…'

143

Geordie guffaws. 'Ha ha! Not a problem. We'd be delighted to help you out. We had no plans for this afternoon, anyway.' *Speak for yourself, you wanker!* I need more information on this little wheeze before I commit.

'How many hay bales?' I ask, suspiciously. Clarence wipes his sweaty head with a handkerchief that is a definite bio threat.

'Not many,' is his vague response, which makes me even more suspicious.

'What exactly does it involve?' I persist with my line of investigation.

He laughs, exposing his blackened stumps. 'Two of you throw bales into the back of the truck. The other two stack them. We take them down to my other hay shed and unload them. Quite simple, really.'

'And how long will this take, exactly?'

'Not long.'

'Come on, boys. It will be fun,' Geordie says as he pulls a shirt on and calls out to his wife. 'Jackie, love! Me and the boys are heading over to Bell End Farm to give Clarence a hand.'

'The mind boggles!' is her curt response from inside the campervan.

'Hang on a mo,' Robbo starts. 'We're being a little hasty, aren't we?' He appears as enamoured with the prospect as I do. Geordie and Clarence are already climbing into the cab.

'That's the problem with you, Robbo. It's all take, take, take. Sometimes in life, you need to put something back. Stop looking out for number one and try giving for a change. You might actually find you enjoy the experience.' Robbo is lost for words. Geordie's propensity for hypocrisy can sometimes catch you off-guard.

'Come on,' Flaky grouses, as he heads towards the truck. 'Let's get it over with.'

'That's the spirit, Flaky,' Geordie encourages. 'Jump up here next to me and Clarence. The self-absorbed twins can ride in the back.'

As the truck makes its way up the dirt track to the farm, Robbo and I are jostled, bumped, and thrown about in the back. To make matters worse, the diesel fumes are intense. The truck pulls up outside a cavernous hay shed, high on a hill overlooking the farmhouse. I'm feeling nauseous.

'I think I've got heavy metal poisoning,' Robbo says as he lowers himself gingerly from the back of the truck. Geordie pushes back a huge roller door, and the truck drives forward. I jump down and stare at the hay bales. I'm not sure how big the barn is but it could definitely house a jumbo jet... maybe two. I notice the forklift truck, abandoned in a corner.

'Not many, you said,' I state, glaring at Clarence.

'Oh, don't worry. We're not moving all of them.'

I breathe a sigh of relief. 'How many?'

'Not many.' Do you ever feel like you're pissing into the wind?

We've been on the go for over three hours and have stopped for a break. Clarence has gone to the farmhouse to fetch us some sustenance and refreshments. My arms and shoulders ache. I'm dripping with sweat. My hands are sore, even though we were all supplied with leather gloves. I lean back on the hay and prepare myself for a marathon whinge.

'What's the bloody point of all this? We've moved about three hundred bales of hay from one barn to another. It's an exercise in futility.'

'You heard what he said,' Geordie replies as he rubs himself down with a towel. 'This is last year's cut. He's emptying this barn so he can store this year's cut.'

'And what's wrong with storing this year's cut in the bloody empty barn near the house.'

'Oh, stop your griping, glass-back. Don't you know that hard work purifies the soul.'

'Thank you, Joseph Stalin,' Robbo grumbles. Geordie flicks him on the arse with the towel.

'Ow! That bloody hurt!'

'It was meant to. With toil comes truth.'

'With toil comes blisters,' Flaky says, inspecting the calluses on his hands.

'What a bunch of wet-nursed, namby-pamby, milksops. You English are all the same,' Geordie sneers. 'Weak as piss!' The clattering of the truck distracts us.

'I wonder what delights he's going to dish up for us?' Flaky ponders glumly.

'Don't expect shucked oysters, caviar and a refreshing dry white,' Robbo says, wincing as he stretches his arms above his head. 'I'm not cut out for this sort of crap. I'm an artist, an intellectual.'

'I've met peanuts with more intellect than you. You should take pride in yourself that you're helping an old farmer in his hour of need,' Geordie chides.

'That's another thing,' I begin. 'What's the bloody rush? Why today, of all days, has he got to move the bloody hay bales? If he gets his forklift fixed, he could move the lot in a couple of hours,' I protest as I glance at my watch. 'It's already five o'clock and we're barely halfway there.' Clarence jumps from the cab in sprightly fashion for a poor old farmer in his dotage. He hauls a picnic hamper onto the ground then pulls a crate full of long-necked beer bottles from the cab.

'Here we go, lads! Tuck in. There's pickled eggs, cold sausage, cheese, and bread. And to wash it all down, my home brewed brown ale. It's a bloody cracking brew if I say so myself.'

'Any water?' Flaky asks. Clarence appears surprised.

'Water? Water's no good for hard work. Did you know the Irish Navvies who built the canals lived on a diet of meat, potatoes, and beer. Not a drop of water in sight. They were the hardest workers this country has ever seen.'

'Really. What was their life expectancy?' Flaky moans. Clarence pulls out four dusty looking pint glasses, fills them up with brown ale and hands them out. I'm always highly suspicious of homebrew. It either tastes like sump oil or gives you galloping gut-rot… or both. This looks different though. It has a creamy appearance with a solid head. Anyway, I'm that thirsty, I could drink anything… even sump oil. I take a hefty draught. It's good. No, it's better than good, it's bloody wonderful! Silence falls over the barn as we all quaff our first pint in record time.

'What do you think?' Clarence asks, smiling at us with his blackened teeth.

'I'll tell you what Clarence,' Geordie begins, 'it's up there with the very best. And I don't say that lightly.'

'I must admit, it's a damn fine ale,' Robbo agrees.

'It has a wonderful complexity of flavours,' Flaky notes. 'Nutty with a hint of sweetness in contrast to a slight bitterness and a satisfying aftertaste.' Clarence refills our glasses as we all attack the food with vigour. Our break lasts a relaxing thirty minutes. We polish off the food and neck down three pints each of brown ale. I'm actually beginning to enjoy myself, as a palpable wave of euphoria washes over me.

'Right, boys, I reckon we can knock this lot over in another couple of hours if we really put our backs into it,' Clarence says as he packs the hamper away and stacks the empty bottles into the beer crate. 'Once we've dropped our last load, I'd like you to sample some of my homemade wine. If it can be grown in England, then I have a wine for it. Elderflower, rhubarb, plum, gooseberry, pear, apple, you name it, and I have it.' I'm looking forward to it.

13: The Payoff

Clarence was right. I'm not sure whether it was the beer or the food, or a combination of both, but we work like Trojans for the next two hours. The mechanic turns up and begins working on the forklift. I'm feeling weary but in a good way. Perhaps, Geordie was right? Hard work *is* good for the soul. However, Clarence's estimated finishing time is well out. There's still a mountain of bales to shift and the Sun is setting. I pull my phone out to ring Fiona. The "no signal" message appears on the screen.

'Clarence, where's the best place to get a signal,' I say holding my mobile up. 'I need to ring the missus.'

'Not around here. You won't get a signal until you get back to the main road. Anyway, we're nearly done. This is the last truckload.' I glance at the huge stack of remaining bales that Robbo is scaling.

'What about those?' I say, nodding towards them. Clarence glances over and spots Robbo's ascent.

'No! Get down from there!' he bellows aggressively. 'They're staying put. They're going to my brother's farm in Ireland.'

'Keep your hair on,' Robbo replies, testily, as he jumps down.

'Come on, get in the truck,' Clarence says, regaining his composure. 'The sooner we get this lot unloaded, the sooner you can sample my wine.' Robbo and I jump into the back and get comfortable on the hay as Flaky climbs into the cab. Geordie saunters over and pulls his mobile out.

'Don't bother,' I shout down to him. 'There's no signal.'

'Geordie!' Clarence calls out. 'Can you close the roller door behind us?'

'Aye, no problem,' he replies as he bends down to tie the lace on his trainer.

Clarence's homemade wine is as good as his homebrew. We're sitting in his cluttered dining room. The place is full of bric-a-brac. Although, according to Clarence, it's not junk. Apparently, rare collector's items and many sought-after relics litter the room. If Clarence is to be believed, which he's not, he's sitting on a small fortune of antiquities. It all looks like crap to me, which should be dumped at the local tip. The only things that appear valuable are the paintings that adorn every wall.

He talks animatedly about his collection. Not that I'm paying much attention as the alcohol has reduced my capacity for concentration and rational thought to that of a lobotomised stick insect. He continually refreshes our glasses. They're not traditional wine glasses. They're shot glasses for reasons he doesn't explain, which I find odd.

There are a dozen or so bottles of wine on the table in front of us, all made from different fruits or vegetables. I must admit, I'm nicely smashed, as we all are... apart from Flaky who is ten sheets to the wind. The only one who appears stone-cold sober is Clarence, who has been matching us glass for glass. The guy must have hollow legs.

As the hours tick by, I've noticed a peculiar trait of Old Clarence. Every time he refills our shot glasses, he picks his glass up and departs to the kitchen. Another round is downed, and Clarence tops us up again. This time I keep one bleary eye on him. To the kitchen he goes, glass in hand.

'This is my favourite—the Elderflower,' he announces with pride. We all lift our glasses in the air. 'Oh, boys,' he says with some excitement, 'you see that painting behind you... the blood red one? It's by an artist called Gerhard Richter.' The other three turn to look, but I keep my focus on Clarence. He quickly pours his wine down the sink.

'That's shite!' Robbo scoffs. 'It's a canvas painted purely in red. Where's the art or skill in that?'

'What do you know about paintings?' Geordie sneers.

'What's it even meant to be?'

'It's abstract art,' Geordie explains. 'It doesn't have to be anything.'

'You mean it's nothing?'

'No, it's not nothing. It can be whatever you want it to be. You enjoy it for what it is.'

'Well, to me, it's shit on a stick,' Robbo huffs.

'That's art,' Clarence begins. 'Art is like beauty—it's in the eye of the beholder. To me, it's beautiful. Come on boys, drink up.' There's a loud rap on the door that startles me. 'That will be the mechanic,' Clarence exclaims as he scurries over to the front door. Muted voices drift through to us. 'Ahem, help yourself to refills, boys. I won't be long,' he shouts. The door slams shut, shortly followed by the unmistakable rumble of his battered truck. I stand up and stare out of the window. The mechanic's van disappears down the farm track whilst the truck makes its way to the top barn. *What is he up to?* I keep my thoughts to myself as I wander around the room. The other three are now in a heated argument about the "red" painting.

I leave the dining room and saunter into the living room. It's a lot tidier. There are two armchairs and a sofa situated around an open fireplace with a small table placed in front of it. Wooden floorboards creak as I tread across them. The room is dusty but cosy enough. I'm about to return to the three cerebral thinkers in the other room when something catches my eye. A large, framed map of the world hangs on a wall. World maps have always held a fascination for me, ever since I was a child. I place a finger on the glass and trace countries out. There are so many I've never heard of, let alone visited… and I'm well-travelled. I come full circle and place my finger on Flexley, then the tiny spur that sticks out into the sea… our campsite. To the south is the river marked with a red dot. Faint pencil dashes plot a route across the Bristol Channel and Celtic Sea to a place in southwest Ireland called, Ballyrean, marked with another red dot. From there, the dashes head due south past Spain and Portugal, hang a left through the Straits of Gibraltar and carry on deep into the Mediterranean, before fading away above North Africa. *That's interesting.* I re-join the others in the dining room.

'You can't splodge paint over a canvas and call it art! That's bullshit!' Robbo yells. It appears the intellectual art discussion continues.

'You have such an 18th century view of the world, don't you?' Flaky says. 'Everyone is entitled to create art. It's not reserved for the so-called geniuses or the elite.'

'I agree everyone is allowed to create it, but whether it's any good is a different matter. If I'd done that painting, you'd all call it out for what it is… self-indulgent shite! It's a case of the Emperor's

New Clothes.' Thankfully, the war of gobbledegook is brought to a premature end as Clarence re-enters the house.

'Sorry, boys, but I'm afraid the party's over,' he announces as Geordie makes a dart for the wine bottle and hurriedly replenishes our glasses. Clarence's demeanour has changed. He appears energised, expectant.

'What's the go?' I ask.

'Just heard from my brother in Ireland and he's desperate for the hay. I'm going to have to load up the barges tonight. They can set sail at dawn.'

'Barges?' I reply.

'Yes. I own two sea barges. They're moored up on the river.'

'Clarence, don't you worry about a thing,' Geordie proclaims. 'Me and the boys will help you out.' *Like hell, we will!* 'It's the least we can do after your gracious hospitality.'

'No, I wouldn't dream of it. The forklift is fixed, and I have men on the barges to help me unload. I'm not willing to take up any more of your time. You've already done more than enough. You must get back to your families. I'll drop you off on the way. Righto, let's go. As a farmer, I'm always fighting time.' Geordie refills the shot glasses one more time before Clarence hurriedly ushers us from the farmhouse. As we stagger towards the truck, I check my watch.

'Holy crap!' I exclaim. 'It's gone 10 pm. We are in the shit. We've been gone over nine hours!' Geordie pats me reassuringly on the shoulder.

'Chill out, Bill. Leave it to me. I have a way with women. I'm an expert in understanding the female psyche. We've done a deed of charity for an ageing farmer. They can't argue with that.'

'I beg to differ.'

'I'll lay out the facts, present our argument, and the case will be dismissed.' I don't share his optimism.

'Don't you think a sincere apology, accompanied with a contrite expression, might work better?'

Geordie sneers. 'What? And give up the moral high ground? Not on your life, sunshine! We've done nothing wrong, in fact, quite the opposite. They cannae argue with logic and reasoning'.

'At 10 o'clock at night, after we've been out most of the day, I'm not sure there's going to be much logic and reasoning.'

'Leave it to your Uncle Geordie. Watch, listen, and inwardly digest.'

'Fine, have it your way.'

'Sweet,' he replies.

Flaky tries three times to climb into the cab but he can barely stand up.

'Look at the state of that wanker,' Geordie curses. 'He's hardly going to help our cause.'

'Come on, we'll lift him into the back. The fresh air will sober him up.' I jump up and grab Flaky's arms as Geordie lifts and heaves him into the back of the truck. He collapses onto the hay bales, muttering incoherently about Gillian and fish.

The truck rocks and rattles its way along the bumpy laneway before turning onto the main road. Flaky is fast asleep as I lay back on the hay and gaze up at the bejewelled inky sky, contemplating life. Ten minutes pass until the truck turns into the campsite and hit's the bloody pothole. There's a loud clank as Flaky and I are jettisoned violently into the air and crash to the floor in a heap. Miraculously, we are unscathed as a couple of hay bales break our fall.

'What the hell was that? Where are we? I must have nodded off,' Flaky says, bewildered by his location in time and space.

'We're at the campsite.' He flops back onto a bale and lets out a deep sigh.

'I don't feel too good.'

'If you don't feel good now, wait until tomorrow. You'll rue the day you were born. You really shouldn't drink, Flaky. You don't have the constitution for it.'

'Thanks for your comforting words,' he grizzles.

'That's what friends are for,' I say absentmindedly. I have more important matters on my mind than a non-smoking, drunken teetotaller. The clanking sound, the hay bales made when we went down the pothole, has piqued my interest. I tap at one of the dislodged bales with the toe of my boot. It meets stiff resistance. I place my hand on it and pull at a thin facade of hay that is attached by string to a wooden crate.

'Hmm... now that's very interesting,' I mumble to myself. Before I have time to investigate further, the truck pulls up next to the motorhomes. I peer through the railings. The scene I witness is to be expected, nonetheless, it does not fill me full of good cheer. Flaky staggers to his feet and peers over the edge with a gormless grin. He waves at them.

'Hello, ladies, you're all looking raving tonight... no, I mean rampaging... no, what I'm trying to say is that you're all beautiful,' he slurs, throwing his arms in the air with an extravagant flourish. He burps, then rushes to the other side of the truck and throws up.

155

*****

For once, Clarence doesn't hang around. His truck labours its way back up the field like an arthritic warthog then hangs a right, towards the river. We all turn around. In front of us are our wives, dressed in pyjamas, arms folded, silent, glaring. They portray a formidable force. I imagine this is how Colonel Custer felt at his last stand, as he realised he should have taken a sick day. Geordie, however, is still full of bonhomie and good-natured optimism. There's none so blind as those who will not see.

'Ah! Jackie, my love, sweetheart, apple of my eye. Now, let me explain…'

'Shut up! You red-nosed, pot-bellied, knock-kneed, splayfooted, windbag! Do you realise you've been absent all day? Fishing in the morning then playing farmers all afternoon and night!' I could be wrong, but I don't think she's in the best of moods.

'Yes, but…'

'Unscrew your neck whilst I'm talking, you chump! By the state you're all in, I'd say there's been more drinking than farming! This was supposed to be a family holiday to spend quality time with your wives and children. You lot have used it as an excuse to get blathered every day.'

Geordie tries to intervene. 'I think that's rather unf…'

'Didn't I tell you to shut your pie hole? Now listen up, you inebriated, slack-jawed, fop-doodles, and listen good!' I'm not sure what a fop-doodle is, but I'm assuming it's not complimentary. 'Tomorrow, us girls are having *our* day off! We'll be departing first thing in the morning and won't be back until late at night… that's if we decide to come back at all. You four nincompoops will be responsible for looking after the children. That means feeding them, watering them, and God forbid, entertaining them. Oh and making sure they're safe. As fathers, I know these things may be alien to you, but I'm sure if you put your collective IQs together you can manage it.'

'I'm not sure I agree, Jackie,' Fiona adds, pithily. 'If they put their collective IQs together, they'd barely make an idiot.' *Christ! This is brutal.*

'No, you're right,' Julie pipes up. 'They can't even look after themselves. They're a shambling shower of shitty, shit, shite.' I'm wondering when Geordie's going to unleash his expertise in understanding the female psyche. He's leaving his run a tad late for my liking.

'I don't feel well,' Flaky moans as he rocks back and forth.

'I'm going to bed now,' Jackie continues. 'Geordie, you can grab your sleeping bag and set it up in the boys' tent, because there's no way I'm having you breathe your toxic alcoholic fumes over me all night.' It appears the "Massacre at Flexley-on-Sea" is drawing to a close. A complete rout by the women. Jackie turns and stomps off. At last, Geordie launches his counteroffensive.

'Yes, dear.' Wow! He gave it to her with both barrels! That told her. Poetry in motion. A sterling defence of our behaviour. He should be a trial lawyer.

'Will, I suggest you clean your teeth and get into bed,' Fiona says as she heads back to the motorhome.

I give her my best sheepish look. 'Okay, love. I'm sorry for all this. We should have known better. Be there in ten.' A thin wisp of a disappointed smile brushes her lips as she turns to me before entering the van.

'Gillian, have I ever told you...' Flaky says as he teeters back and forth, 'ever told you... how... how...'

'Yes, Flaky, what are you trying to say?' Gillian replies, with her understanding, caring, and forgiving manner.

'How much... I love your fish pie.'

'Is that a euphemism?' Robbo giggles as he attempts to roll a joint.

'You're a disgusting, little pothead,' Julie snarls at her husband. 'I'm so disappointed in you.'

'What's new?' he replies, without a care in the world.

Julie massages her forehead. 'I thought you wanted to change. You were going to give up the booze and dope and get yourself fit. The fact is, you can't, not when you're in your natural environment. I hope this stint on the TV show, isolated, cut off from your crutches, gives you time to reflect. It will either make or break you. I hope for your sake... for our sakes, it's the former, because I'm getting a little tired of going through these peaks and troughs. Come to bed when you want... or don't come at all. I really don't care anymore.' Another wife disappears into the campervan. Gillian leads Flaky by the arm towards their abode.

'I'll get you a glass of electrolyte and some paracetamol,' she whispers. 'But you're still going to have a terrible hangover tomorrow. You know how drinking doesn't agree with you. You've been very silly.'

'I know. I'm a Silly Billy,' he sniggers. 'We had been working very hard. It wasn't all about drinking,' he slurs, as his wobbly boots guide him home. Only Robbo, Geordie and me are left standing. Suitably chastised, flagellated, publicly embarrassed we should clamber quietly into our cots and head to the land of nod. But there's one cockwomble who has other ideas.

'Right, boys, how about a couple of refreshing beers to dilute the wine before we hit the sack?' Geordie whispers. I'm a grown man with responsibilities. His suggestion is completely out of order after the day we've had and the justified admonishment we've received from our spouses.

'Okay. In for a penny, in for a pound,' I respond, wearily.

'Good man. You grab a six-pack from the cooler, and we'll head down to the cliffs. Give me a minute to move my sleeping bag and grab something from the car.' Amazingly, or maybe not, Robbo has managed to roll a spliff and loses no time in sparking up.

'Nice night,' he drawls, staring at the twinkling stars in the dark sky.

'Yes, it is. Well, apart from…'

'Apart from the ear-bashing?'

'Yeah.'

'Ah, don't worry about it. They'll have forgotten by tomorrow.' Robbo's nonchalance doesn't reassure me. The girls seemed pretty pissed off to me. The last thing I need in the morning, sporting a cracking hangover, is chaperoning five energetic and excitable kids. Geordie reappears and motions for us to follow him. Once we are safely out of earshot of the campervans, I twist the tops off three beers and hand them out.

'One more after this then it's time for bed,' I emphatically state.

'Aye, spot on, Billy Boy. Everything in moderation,' he says as he throws the beer down his neck.

'Oh, by the way. That was a brilliant defence you put up back there.'

He grins. 'Aye. One of my best. You see, the thing is, you need to think like your opponent thinks. Initially, I was going to talk about all the hard work we'd done, you know, lending a helping hand to a farmer on the rails. Then it came to me in a blinding flash of clarity.'

'What did?' Robbo asks.

'The Muhammed Ali fight against George Foreman, the "Thriller in Manilla". I used the same tactics.'

'I think it was the "Rumble in the Jungle", but don't let me interrupt.'

Geordie gives me a disapproving glance. 'As I was saying… after the first round, Ali knew he couldn't go toe to toe with Foreman, so he changed tactics. He tucked into the ropes and protected his body and head. Foreman pounded him for round after round but became exhausted. Then, in the last round, Ali unleashed hell and knocked Foreman out.'

'Ah, I see,' Robbo begins. 'Just one small observation, though.'

'What's that?'

'We were still on the ropes getting the shit kicked out of us as the final bell rang. I think the girls won a unanimous points decision,' Robbo says as he necks his beer.

'You think so?' Geordie murmurs as he scratches his cheek.

'I know so. It was a bloodbath.'

'And the worst is yet to come,' I add. 'Tomorrow we have the children to attend to—all day.'

Geordie snorts. 'Stuff and nonsense. You forget; I understand the inner workings of the female mind. There's no way those women are going to disappear for the day and leave us in charge. They're playing a game of psychological bluff, cat and mouse, and I'm onto it. We'll outmanoeuvre them, you wait and see. They're full of wind and piss. Sound and fury is their name! I'm the master of the long game.' I can't be bothered to argue with the muppet. I only hope he's right.

As we near the fence line of the field, Geordie pulls two tubes out of his back pocket.

'What are those?' I ask.

'You'll see, soon enough.' He fiddles about with one of them before tugging at a string. There's an instant "whooshing" sound and a burst of blinding light.

'You dickhead!' I shout. 'Please tell me that's not a firework?'

'Calm down, Billy Boy,' he says, grinning as he repeats the process with the second tube. 'They're parachute distress flares which have passed their use-by date.' The second flare follows a similar trajectory to the first and bursts into a dazzling luminescent star. They glide languidly down towards the sea, carving a streaky red glow into the silhouette of the night.

'That's what you call a bit of light entertainment. And for the encore we can watch the launch of the lifeboat and the arrival of the air-sea-rescue helicopter,' Robbo says as he puffs on his spliff. The stupid smirk falls from Geordie's face.

'Nah… you don't think so, do you?' he says, rubbing at the stubble on his chin.

'They're distress flares. That's what they're designed for,' I reply.

'Shit! Come on, we better call it a night,' Geordie says as he grabs another beer and heads back up the hill. A distant flash of white light is followed a few seconds later by the rumble of thunder.

'Looks like there's a storm heading our way,' Robbo says as he stamps his joint out. I glance at Geordie's disappearing figure, then at Robbo, and sigh.

'How old is he,' I quiz, rhetorically.

'Physically, he's recently turned forty. Mentally, he's fifteen, always has been, always will be.'

14: The Hangover

The four of us stare disconsolately at the back of the Range Rover as it makes its way up the hill. Three quick blasts from the car's horn briefly interrupts the distant sound of an Abba song. The vehicle passes through the campsite entrance, turns left and disappears from view. It's 7:35 am, and I have the Chernobyl of hangovers.

'Daddy, I'm hungry,' Mary calls out as she appears on the campervan steps rubbing her eyes.

'They did that on purpose,' Geordie grumbles with a pained expression.

'What?' Robbo asks.

'Blowing the bloody car horn to make sure they woke all the kids up. That's a dirty, underhand tactic. Those women don't fight fair.'

'And sound and fury is their name,' Robbo states with a hint of irony.

'Yep, full of wind and piss,' I concur.

Geordie growls at us. 'Perhaps they'll be back in an hour or two once they've made their point.'

'Something tells me not. Call it my sixth sense working overtime. Or perhaps it was when Jackie called you a lumbering, moronic, fucknut, and not to make dinner for them, as they'd be eating out,' I explain.

'Da! Da! Can you tell Wallace off! He farted in my face!' Robert cries from the confines of his tent. He scrambles through the opening, squeezing his nostrils together. 'Holy shite! That's bloody rank. You dirty bastard!'

'That's rather colourful language for a six-year-old.' It's the first words Flaky has spoken since he awoke. He looks like death warmed up.

'Robert! I don't want to hear any more swear...' Geordie stops abruptly, mid-sentence, as his shoulders heave violently upwards. He clutches at the back of his head with eyes scrunched tightly shut. 'Christ almighty! Where's the archer hiding?'

'The archer?' Robbo queries.

'Yeah, some bastard just fired a burning arrow into the back of my fucking skull.'

'Daddy, did you hear me? I'm hungry. What's for breakfast?'

'Yes! I heard you, Mary. I'll make scrambled eggs on toast in a minute.'

'But I don't like scrambled eggs. I want tomato soup.' I'd normally put my foot down at her ridiculous request, so early in the morning... but what the hell.

'Okay. Tomato soup it is.'

'Ooh! Goody. I'll see if Katrina and Sally want tomato soup.' Through narrow slits, I peer at my mates.

'The D-Day landings were coined, "The Longest Day." They were wrong. Today is going to be—the longest day.'

Of course, none of the children can agree on the same thing for breakfast, so Geordie and I end up making five different meals. We wouldn't tolerate this under normal circumstances, but these are not normal circumstances. With the use of pained expressions and grimaces, as our universal language, we conclude it's the lesser of two evils. No one is up for arguments or tantrums today.

With breakfast pots cleared away, the children are becoming restless. It's barely gone 8 am.

'Dad, can we go to the funfair again?' Robert asks.

'Not today, son. We're having a nice quiet one around the campsite.'

'Oh, but it's boring,' Wallace complains. 'We want excitement and adventure.'

'Excitement and adventure are overrated. You can have that tomorrow. Today you're having, "boring". Believe me, boring can be quite enjoyable, sometimes.'

'But aren't we going home tomorrow?' Wallace exclaims.

'Wallace, stop shouting and asking so many questions. Your father's feeling a little delicate this morning. If you want adventure, you can hang that basket of washing out,' Geordie grimaces. His suggestion closes down the conversation with his son.

'Uncle Will,' Katrina says as she pulls at my shirt sleeve. 'Will you play a game of hide and seek with us?'

'Yes, yes,' Sally and Mary agree in unison.

'No. I've got something far better than that. Arts and crafts.' The girls look doubtful, and Geordie's lads look mortified.

'Not bloody arts and crafts again!' Wallace cries.

'Wallace, language!' Geordie shouts, before clutching at his head. 'Suckering suckerfish,' he mutters.

'You'll like this arts and crafts,' I say, trying to sound positive despite suspecting an aneurism is but one raised voice away.

'What is it?' Sally asks.

'I have giant ceramic eggs and paints. Now, you run along and spread newspaper over the table, and I'll get the eggs.' The kids seem intrigued. I make my way to the campervan, stepping over Robbo's prostrate, lifeless body, laid out on a picnic blanket. 'Robbo?'

'What?'

'Nothing. Just making sure you haven't died. It's going to be another warm day and cadavers go off pretty quickly in the heat. I don't want you puffing up and exploding. It would be a hell of a mess to clean up and I've got enough on my plate.'

'I'll let you know when I'm dead. I don't want to cause any fuss.'

'Cheers.'

I return with the box of large ceramic eggs and paint set. As I place them on the table, the children become enthused.

'Wow!' Wallace exclaims. 'They're like dinosaur eggs.'

'Cool,' Sally gushes. 'I'm going to paint a face on mine.'

'Right, you have three each. And don't rush them. Good artwork takes time, a very long time, in fact, at least three hours. Study the picture on the box and see how beautiful and intricate you can make them.' The kids all gawp at the illustration on the box. I leave them to it and return to my camp chair.

'How long do you give them?' Geordie inquires.

'Your lads, about fifteen minutes. The girls, half-hour, max. Flaky, stick the kettle on and make us all a brew, will you?' He doesn't respond. 'Flaky?' He puts a finger to his lips.

'Shush. Please, no shouting.'

'I wasn't shouting.'

'There you go again.'

'This is no good,' I sigh. 'I have a plan.'

'Not one of your bloody infamous plans,' Robbo grizzles.

'Go on, Bill. Any plan has got to be better than this hellish nightmare.'

'It's called Operation Staggered Fathering.'

'Operation Shaggered Fathering would be a better name,' Robbo yawns. I ignore his barb and continue.

'There's no point in us all sitting here suffering. I suggest we set up a shift system. I'll do the first hour on duty, and you lot can go back to bed. After an hour, I'll hand over to Robbo, and I'll go back to bed. Robbo hands over to Geordie, and Geordie you hand over to Flaky to do the last shift.' The response is underwhelming.

'Hang on, how come Mr Lightweight gets the last shift? That means he gets three hours sleep,' Geordie moans.

'We all get three hours sleep. And Flaky goes last because… well, look at the state of him. He looks like dog vomit.'

'Aye, and he doesnae smell much better. Okay, it's a good idea. Another three hours kip should have me firing on all cylinders again,' he says, already making his way back to his tent. Robbo rises unsteadily to his feet and plods up the steps of his van, as Flaky disappears inside his. Right, now for that cup of tea.

I was right about the egg painting. Within fifteen minutes, Wallace had finished his three eggs. A rugby ball, a dinosaur egg, and his masterpiece, a hand grenade. His brother, obviously devoid of any other ideas, copied him. The girls fared a lot better and produced some charming artwork. Sally's eggs were especially delicate and beautiful. She used pastel colours to paint the whole egg, then enhanced them with delicate patterns of white. She's definitely inherited her mother's artistic bent.

I decide to take them all to the beach, not because I'm a good father, but for my own ulterior, selfish reasons. First off, they all have paint over their hands, arms, and faces, plus a good dollop or two in their hair. The thought of scrubbing paint off five whining kids is not something my throbbing head can take. I figure that forty minutes running in and out of seawater and rolling about in sand will do the job for me. Second, a fresh sea breeze may alleviate my hangover symptoms. And lastly, I can sit in the sand and bark instructions to them as I organise races and tag teams. This will burn off some of their energy, meaning that this afternoon they'll all take a little nap… maybe. I live in hope.

*****

My one hour stint has ballooned into two hours, and I'm in desperate need of some shuteye and a head transplant. I knock on Robbo's door and let myself in.

'Oi, Robbo! You're on duty.' He's sprawled out on the bed, fully clothed. The place stinks to high heaven, so I quickly throw open a few windows. He groans as he lifts his head slightly to peer at me.

'No way, man! I've only just laid down. That can't be an hour already.'

'No, you're right. It's two hours. Now shift your lazy arse and supervise the kids. I'm hitting the hay.'

'Christ, don't mention hay. I've been having nightmares about the bloody stuff.' I grab him by the arm, pull him to his feet and steer him down the steps. The children are sitting around sipping on chilled lemonade. I make my way to my campervan and close the door behind me. As I drop yet another electrolyte tablet into a glass of water and reach for the paracetamol, I can hear Robbo try to assert his authority.

'Right, gang, listen up! For the next hour, we're all going to sit quietly and read a book.' A chorus of disapproval greets his suggestion.

'No way!' Wallace screams. 'I'm not reading no bloody book! I want adventure and excitement.'

'Well, read Treasure Island, then. Don't give me any grief, Wallace.'

'You can't tell me what to do. You're not my dad!' I put the tablets in my mouth, slurp down the electrolyte, close all the windows and fall onto the bed. Within seconds, the mutiny outside fades as blessed sleep consumes me.

*****

I rouse from slumber as the mouthwatering aroma of fried bacon sizzling on the barbeque assails my nostrils. Subdued talking filters through to the inside of the van. I make my way outside and stretch. A scene of domestic harmony greets me. I pinch myself. No, it's definitely not a dream. The children are halfway down the field, flying kites. Geordie is manning the hotplate.

'Ah, the Kraken wakes. You ready for breakfast, Bill?' Geordie asks.

'What's the time?'

'Just after 1 pm.'

'Yeah, a bacon and egg roll would go down great guns.'

'There's a fresh brew of coffee in the pot,' Robbo states as he sparks up a reefer and plonks down in his chair with a large mug of coffee. I glance to his left. Slumped in his camp chair, with shades on and a wet towel draped around his neck, is Flaky.

'I feel better for that sleep,' I state.

'Yeah, me too. Good idea of yours,' Geordie says. 'Credit where credit's due. The rest of the day will be a breeze. I can't wait until the women get home. The looks on their faces, when they realise there's been no disasters or calamities, will be worth its weight in gold. They think we're incapable, but we've proved them wrong. Underestimate the four musketeers at your...' he stops and glances disdainfully at Flaky. 'Underestimate the three musketeers at your own peril. We can survive anything. Onwards and upwards.'

'Christ, Geordie, all we're doing is looking after our own children for the day. It's hardly the advance on Stalingrad,' I respond.

'In its own small way, it is,' he says as he takes a huge mouthful of a bacon and egg butty. 'That was the Mount Everest of all hangovers,' he mumbles as bits of food fly from his mouth. 'At one point I could swear I was having a stroke. But I've got to say, I'm coming good now. Still bloody stiff from shifting those hay bales, though. In another couple of hours, I reckon I'll be ready for a hair-of-the-dog. Flaky, you up for a fried egg sandwich?'

Flaky groans. 'You must be joking. Even the smell of the bacon is making me dry retch. I'm not sure how you can eat. I don't think I'll ever eat again.' Geordie shakes his head in a disappointed fashion.

'There's always one who lets the team down. You better smarten your ideas up before the women arrive back. We don't want any traitors in the ranks when we're quizzed about our day. It's all been easy-peasy-lemon-squeezy, do you understand?'

'Shut up and leave me alone,' he murmurs.

'Why do you always have to take a confrontational view of life?' Robbo asks as he sips on his brew.

'Because, sunshine, life is a constant battle. A battle against disease, illness, arseholes, dickhead friends, and passive-aggressive wives. It's a battle every one of us will ultimately lose… but a battle, nonetheless. And until my dying breath, I will march onwards into the breach, with a Claymore in my left hand, a Targe in my right, and a beating bloodied heart in the other.'

'Oh, you have three hands now, do you? One of them containing a beating heart.' Flaky mumbles.

'Don't come the Smart Alec with me! You know what I mean. Never let your guard down. That's all I'm saying. Here, Bill, your bacon and egg roll is ready to go.'

'Cheers,' I reply gratefully as I bite into it.

'Flaky, are you sure I can't tempt you with a greasy fried egg sandwich?' Geordie inquires, quite deliberately.

'Bugger off!'

15: The Mystery

The food and coffee have worked their magic, and I'm feeling a little better. It's incremental, but at least my headache is retreating at the speed of a glacier.

'Have any of you lot seen my mobile phone?' Geordie asks. We all shake our heads. 'I've searched high and low for the damn thing.' I pull out my mobile and call him.

'Everyone, quiet,' I say.

'I can't hear it,' Geordie murmurs.

'Did you leave it in the Range Rover?' Flaky says as he takes another hearty swig of water.

'Hmm… possibly.'

'When was the last time you had it?' I quiz him.

'Let me think,' he says as he closes his eyes. I stare at him as the rusty cogs in his head grind slowly around. I try to help him out.

'The last time I saw you with it was yesterday in the barn, as we finished loading the last of the hay bales onto the truck. You pulled it out to make a call but there was no signal; remember?'

'Aye! You're right. And I placed it on the ground as I bent down to tie my lace. That's where it'll be. I hope Clarence didn't run over the bloody thing. I best get up there and try to find it.'

'I'll go with you.'

'Okay, we'll take your campervan.'

'No. Let's walk. It will brush away the cobwebs.'

'Walk!' he exclaims as though I'd suggested self-amputation of a limb. 'I'm as stiff as an old boot after that bloody workout yesterday. And do you trust Shagnasty and Pencil Dick to look after the kiddies whilst we're gone?'

'I'm coming good at an exponential rate,' Robbo responds. It's true. Earlier this morning he couldn't even face a spliff. Now he's going for it with gusto.

'Exponentially high. You'll be up there with the bloody kids' kites if you have another one.'

'Geordie, they'll be fine. It will be a nice, pleasant stroll. Just the thing your body needs to ease the aches and pains. Trust me, I do a lot of walking and it always revives me. It's not that far, maybe 30 to 40 minutes give or take.' He looks unconvinced but reluctantly agrees.

'Aye, okay. You get a backpack and a couple of bottles of water. I'll let the boys know that I'll be gone for a while.' He turns and heads towards the children.

'Flaky, Robbo, make sure you keep an eye on the kids,' I implore.

Flaky moves his head about a millimetre. 'Will do. I don't intend to move from this chair until my head stops throbbing. But I will keep my eye on them.'

'Robbo?' I nag.

'Yeah, yeah… everything's cool, man. I reckon the kids will be ready for a bit of quiet time soon. They've been on the go since they first got up. All's good. You and Geordie go on your lovers walk together. You can rest assured, on our watch, the kids are in safe hands.'

'Good man,' I reply as I grab my backpack and head to the campervan to refill two water bottles.

Instead of following the main road to the farm track we take a shortcut and climb over a stone wall and drop into a field. The farmhouse is nothing but a dot in the distance, and I realise it's further than I estimated. I also notice, that as the crow flies, it's directly opposite the campsite albeit a few miles away.

It's another stunning day with clear, ice-blue skies. A gentle spring breeze carries an invigorating earthy odour on its wings. The rain, from the previous night, has brought a new verve and lustre to the countryside. A skylark, high above but unseen, sings a frenetic lullaby. I slip into a reverie as the subdued buzz of insects and the distant bleat of sheep sedates me, pushing troubled thoughts to the back of my mind.

After thirty minutes of walking, we stop to laze under the shade of an oak tree and refresh ourselves with thirsty gulps of water.

'So much for a half hour's walk,' Geordie moans as he gazes up at the farmhouse which is still some way off.

'I'm glad. I'm enjoying the serenity. There's no better place in the world than England when the weather's nice.' I pull out a chocolate bar, snap a few blocks off and pass them to Geordie.

'Ah, that's the ticket. A hit of glucose. Good thinking.' We fall silent. My conscious mind has returned and is turning over the events

175

that have occurred since we arrived. The crate in the truck isn't the only peculiar occurrence that has aroused my curiosity.

'As much as I could sit here all day, we best get a move on. It's not fair to leave Flaky and Robbo in charge for so long.'

'I suppose you're right. So, what's on your mind, Bill?' Geordie asks.

'On my mind?'

He chuckles. 'I've known you long enough to spot the signs.' I drop the water into the backpack, zip it up and rise to my feet.

'Do you really want to know?'

'Of course, I do.'

'You'll think I'm an idiot.'

'If it looks like a duck, swims like a duck and quacks like a duck,' he chuckles.

'I don't think your pal Clarence is all he's cracked up to be.'

'What do you mean? He's simply an old-time farmer trying to get by. He's a little eccentric, I'll give you that. But he's harmless.'

'That's what he wants the world to think, and he's done a good job of fooling everyone. It's how the barman at The Railway, and Sergeant Waygood, see him. Probably all the locals.'

'But not you. Go on then, spit it out.'

'Let's start with the campsite. Apart from us and Twitchy, there are no other campers. I mean, really? It's Easter, for God's sake. Even if he is a tight-arse and doesn't want to spend money on advertising, why wouldn't he have made a sign for the campsite entrance? Even something simple. A placard with "Camping Vacancies" painted on it and a telephone number.'

'I don't follow your argument. Your inference is that he doesn't want campers. If that were the case, then why are we there?'

'To make it look like he *does* want campers.'

'Christ, Bill, even trying to figure out what that means is twisting my melon.'

'I'll come back to it later. Next—the fishing trip. We were supposed to go a couple of miles offshore and we ended up near Lands End. We drop our lines in for an hour, the speedboat pulls up, two guys climb aboard, then it's lines in and anchor up. The only explanation Bubbles gave was that a storm was on its way. It was a perfect day, not a cloud in sight.'

'Hang on, back up. There was a storm later that night.'

'Twelve hours later. Hardly imminent, was it?'

'And what has this got to do with Clarence?'

'It's his boat. Bubbles works for Clarence.'

'How do you know that?'

'He told me and Robbo the day we took the kids to the animal farm. Moving on, those hay bales yesterday, it was a farce.'

'Why?'

'First off, why would he ask four musicians, who have never done a hard day's work in their life, to help him with an onerous manual labouring job. He's been here all his life and would know every local within a thirty-mile radius. Why didn't he ask another farmer to lend him their farmhands for a day or even borrow someone's forklift? And why was it so imperative to move them yesterday? Why didn't he wait until the mechanic had fixed his forklift? It took five of us six hours, that's thirty-man hours, to shift that load. A forklift would have done the job in two hours, max. We moved over a thousand hay bales from one giant barn up on a hill to another giant barn further down near the farmhouse. What was the point of it?'

'He explained that.'

'Yes, I know, and it was a piss poor excuse. He said he wanted to free up the top barn for this year's hay cut.'

'If you don't believe him, then what's your explanation?'

'I'll come to that in a moment. So, we move all the bales, bar about a thousand, from one barn to another. When we asked why he was leaving those bales behind he said he was transporting them to his brother who has a farm on the east coast of Ireland. We had a wet winter and a warm spring. The grass is growing rampant. I'm sure it's the same in Ireland. Why would his brother need hay at this time of year?'

'Och, who knows the ways of farmers. How do you know his brother hasn't increased his herd and is going to be short of grass? It could be any number of reasons.'

'All right, let's move on from the hay moving debacle. Last night he got us pissed, deliberately. At first, I thought he was being friendly and appreciative of our gruelling work. Each time he refilled our glasses, and his own, he'd disappear behind the kitchen counter then point to some object or painting on the wall.'

'Can't say I noticed, but he was up and down a lot. Those old guys who work non-stop are like that; they don't know how to relax and switch off.'

'I didn't spot it myself until later in the night. It suddenly hit me it was odd behaviour. So, the next time he did the refills I watched him. Behind the kitchen counter, he went. He pointed at the red painting on the wall. The rest of you all turned your heads to look, but I didn't. He went to the kitchen sink and poured his drink away.'

'He's an old man. Perhaps he can't hold his drink anymore but wants to appear like he's one of the lads.'

'Maybe. Then the mechanic knocks on the door and says he's finished repairing the forklift. Clarence tells us he won't be long and drives up to the top barn, loads the truck up and returns to the farmhouse. He said he'd just spoken with his brother in Ireland who desperately needed the hay. How?'

'How what?'

'How did he speak to his brother? There's no mobile signal on the farm. We know that ourselves.'

'Carrier pigeon?'

I disregard his facetious comment. 'Then, suddenly, it's time for him to drop us back at the campsite.'

'Well, we were all smashed by that time. You're overthinking things, jumping at shadows. You had it in for Clarence from day one and don't you deny it.'

'I didn't have it in for him. I didn't like him, that's true. He's a lustful old perv. But this is different.'

'I'm an expert judge of character and I can tell he's a good egg.'

'No, he's a bad egg and you're a terrible judge of character! Remember the time we toured the States, and you befriended that guitar roadie, Woody? You thought the sun shone out of his arse. You invited him along to all the showbiz parties and were always hanging out with him, and what did he do? Halfway through the tour, he does a disappearing act with all our guitars and Robbo's bag of amphetamines.'

He chuckles. 'I'd forgotten about that. My most vivid memory was the look of terror on Robbo's face when we broke the news to him.'

'I'm not surprised. He lost a lot of classic guitars.'

'It wasn't that. It was the loss of his speed that nearly finished him off. I thought I was going to have to ring for an ambulance.' We stop walking as I light a smoke. 'Anyway, Miss Marple, have you finished your character assassination of Clarence?'

'Nearly.'

'I'm not sure I want to hear anymore. If I were a judge, I'd throw this one out of court. All you have on him is opinion, presumption, and circumstantial evidence.'

'Not quite.'

'Strewth!'

'I'll proceed to the next anomaly. Last night, as we drove through the campground entrance, the truck went down that pothole.'

'Tell me about it. I hit my bloody noggin on the roof of the cab. He needs to get that hole filled in. It's a menace, a real bone shaker.'

'You were lucky! It jolted all the hay bales into the air, and I nearly fell out of the truck.'

'It's hardly the crime of the century, is it? Going down a pothole.'

'No, it's not about the pothole it's about the sound the hay bales made as they landed.'

'Sound?'

'They clanked.'

'Clanked.'

'Yes, clanked.'

'What does that mean?'

'You know what a clank is. A jangle, a clang, a clatter, a crash.'

'Don't talk daft. Hay bales don't clank.'

'Exactly. The row of hay bales at the back, which Flaky and me were sitting on, were genuine. I lifted one up and felt at the one below. It had a facade of hay as a covering, but it wasn't a hay bale.'

'What was it?'

'A wooden crate.'

'A wooden crate.'

I glare at him. 'Are you deliberately trying to annoy me?'

'Pardon me for breathing. What was in this crate?'

'Unfortunately, I'd forgotten to bring my crowbar with me, so I couldn't tell you.'

'So what? Maybe Clarence is a bit of an old rogue, a rascal, but he's harmless. He has a keen interest in antiques. Perhaps he's a counterfeiter of relics, collectables. Ireland would be the perfect stopping off point to smuggle them into the States. The Yanks love that sort of shit, you know, pieces of old British antiquity. It's not really harming anyone, is it?' I stub my cigarette out as we stroll on. The farmhouse is clearly discernible now. We make a detour to the right to bypass the house and head directly to the upper barn.

'I haven't finished yet,' I say.

'Strike a light! This is longer than Bleak House… and about as much fun.'

'Last night I woke about 2 pm—hot, sweaty, dehydrated. I drank some water, then went outside for a cigarette. Everyone had their van windows open, so I walked down towards the cliff, so the smoke didn't drift inside the vans. There was the rumble of thunder in the distance and the occasional flash of lightning. I'd nearly finished my cig when the wind picked up in a matter of seconds. A moment later, a massive flash of sheet lightning lit the whole place up. For three or four seconds, it was daylight. Like someone had flicked on a lightbulb. That's when I spotted it. I don't know why, but it sent an icy chill down my back.'

'You're beginning to freak me out. Spotted what?'

'A small boat or dinghy out to sea, with two people in it, near to the cliff. The rain came, and I hightailed it back to the van. I tried to sleep but was restless, plus the storm really kicked off. Something is comforting about a storm when you're safe and warm under the blankets. It didn't last long, maybe twenty, thirty minutes. About an hour passed, and I was feeling sleepy. The storm had moved back out to sea. An occasional flash lit up the sky, followed by the rumble of thunder, but it was heading away from us. I reached that point where you're not awake, but neither are you asleep. It's like a blissful layby between two worlds. Then I heard male voices, hushed but agitated. I jumped out of bed, checked the lock on the door and grabbed a carving knife from the drawer, before flicking off the nightlight that we leave on for Mary. I stared out of the window, but it was pitch black and I couldn't see a thing. When another flash of lightning lit up the place... I spotted them. Two men heading towards our camp. I'm not sure what language they were speaking, but it wasn't English.'

'You must have some idea. Was it Asian, French, German?'

'No. It was Eastern European. Possibly Russian.'

'Did you see their faces?'

'No. There was another flash, and they stopped dead in their tracks. They'd noticed the campervans for the first time. They dropped to their haunches, made hand signals to each other, then bolted sideways across the field away from us. They appeared more scared than I was. I grabbed the knife, went outside, waited, and listened. After a few minutes, I spotted them as they made their way out of the entrance to the campground. They headed left, down the main road, towards Flexley. That was the last I saw of them.'

'Don't tell me... you think they were the two men you saw in the dinghy and possibly the same men who came aboard the fishing charter?'

'It's not such a long bow to draw. Bit of a coincidence, don't you think?'

'I'll tell you what I think; I was quite enjoying this holiday until you started with all this cloak and dagger nonsense. It's put the willies up me. So, what's your theory?'

'I know Clarence was using the real hay bales in the barn to cover up the fake ones. If you wanted to hide a needle, where would you hide it?'

'In a haystack?'

'No, you'd hide it with another thousand needles, in plain sight but out of sight. I also know he had a deadline to meet last night. That's why he enlisted our help. We're out-of-towners and will be leaving in two days time. He didn't want any locals getting suspicious, as they would have done moving bales from one shed to another for no apparent reason.'

'And the two mystery men?' We clamber over a stone wall and drop onto soft springy grass.

'That's what I'm not sure about.'

'They could be artisans, you know, craftsmen who can reproduce exact replicas of antiques.'

'Possibly. Or perhaps they're nothing to do with Clarence. It's possible Bubbles has got a sideline in people smuggling. Come on, the sooner we get to the barn, the sooner we'll find out what's in those crates.'

'And how do you intend to get them open?' I unzip my backpack and pull out a tyre lever, borrowed from the campervan.

'With this,' I say, grinning at him.

'You crafty bastard. That's called going equipped.'

16: The Barn

From the vantage point of the upper barn, we have a perfect view of the farmhouse and outbuildings below.

'I can't see his truck,' I say, scanning the farmyard.

'No, nor me. He's probably out and about.'

'Hmm… good. Gives us a bit more time.'

We push the roller door back a little and enter the cavernous hay shed. It's murky, but soft filtered light floods in from gaps at the top of the tin gables high above, creating a spotlight on the ground. It illuminates a choreographed, languid dance of microscopic dust. The gentle buzz of flies is the only sound. The air smells as sweet as honey from the desiccated grass. It's warm and peaceful. I feel a temporary sense of comfort. On the back wall is the stack of hay bales Clarence told us not to touch the day before. They're about ten high and a dozen deep. It looks like he only moved one load last night and probably abandoned any further haulage activities when the storm arrived. I feel scared but excited at the same time.

'Right, let's find my bloody phone, take a quick butchers in a crate, then get out of here. We're technically trespassing,' Geordie says as he makes his way to the approximate spot where the truck was last parked. I retrieve the tyre iron, throw the backpack into a corner, and head to the back wall. Bad tempered chuntering echoes around the barn as Geordie searches for his mobile. I walk along the front of the stacked bales and bang the tyre iron against them. Each one offers stiff resistance as the metal bar slams through the thin camouflage into wood.

'Told you, Geordie. They're crates dressed up as hay bales. I'm going to climb on top to open one up,' I shout out to him.

'Never mind about the bloody crates, come and help me look for my phone!' The bales are about fourteen feet in height but thankfully they're stacked on wooden pallets, four bales high, making it easy to scale. I stick the tyre iron down the back of my pants then clamber up. 'Ah! Here we go, found it!' Geordie exclaims. 'The battery's dead but there's no sign of damage.'

'I'm glad about that,' I mumble under my breath as I pull my micro-pocketknife out, extract the blade and cut through three strands of twine, which hold the hay disguise in place. I jam the tyre lever into the top edge of the crate and give it a thwack with the ball of my thumb. Geordie's theory about fake antiques could be on the money. I guess there's a first time for everything. I'm hoping he's correct then I can forget about everything and get back to enjoying my holiday. If Clarence is ripping off wealthy Americans with his replica relics, what do I care? The wooden lid creaks and groans as I work the tyre leaver along the outer edge. I repeat the process until the cover pops off. I stare into the box. There's more hay inside, covering the contents. I push it aside.

'Holy shite,' I whisper as my heartbeat accelerates so fast, I forget to breathe, causing a momentary dizzy spell. My mouth is dry and a steady trickle of sweat runs down my back.

'You'd think in this day and age a phone battery would last longer than 24 hours. This bloody thing cost me over £600! I think I'll take it back and get them to replace the battery. I must have got a dud. What have you found up there?' Geordie calls out as he walks towards the bales. 'Anything interesting? I bet I was right, wasn't I? I have a nose for these things. It's called lateral thinking. You may have spotted the clues, but it takes real brains in solving a mystery. We should open a private detective agency. We could call it the Cluesome Twosome or Double Trouble Detective Agency. What do you think about that?' I wish the moron would shut the fuck up, that's what I think. I'm trying to calm my flight or fight response, which has gone into overdrive, and his jovial, inane banter is not helping matters. I feel nauseous and realise I've let my curiosity get the better of me and put us all at risk. The bales rock gently as Geordie climbs up. I pull one assault rifle from the crate and hold it away from my body. My hands shake violently. Geordie's oversized melon pops up above the bales to be met with the barrel of the gun.

'Argh!' he screams as he disappears. There's a thump as he hits the dirt below. 'You bloody idiot! Don't you know not to point guns at people!' He doesn't seem as jovial as he was a second ago. 'Is that thing loaded?' I inspect the rifle but know nothing about guns. I try to keep away from them. As Fiona said, a few days ago, they're nothing but trouble.

'I don't think so. I can't see one of those bullet gizmos.'

'It's called a magazine, you clown! Put the bloody thing down, I'm coming back up! I know a thing or two about military guns.'

'How come?' I ask, slightly sceptical.

'When I was at school…'

'I should have guessed. The number of things you did at school is quite remarkable. You must have been a student for over fifty years.'

'As I was saying, when I was at school,' he repeats, clearly annoyed, 'we spent a day at an army barracks. It was a sort of recruitment drive. We tackled the assault course and later went into a classroom and studied guns that different armies from around the world use.' He pulls himself up and snatches the rifle from me. 'Jesus H fucking tapdancing Christ in a taxicab!' he exclaims. 'It's an AK-47 or some variant of it.' He peers inside the crate. 'Kiss my sweet hairy arse until judgement day. There must be a dozen in each box!'

'And if each bale is full of rifles, that's about 1200 of the buggers, not to mention the ones he loaded onto the truck last night.'

'No, they won't all be full of rifles, maybe half will. The others will be full of magazines. No point in having a gun if you don't have any bullets. Looks like Sergeant Waygood was right about old Clarence.'

'What do you mean?' I ask as he studies the rifle with unwarranted admiration.

'He said he could get up to mischief.'

'Mischief!' I yell, flabbergasted at his statement. 'Mischief is knocking on doors and running away, fiddling your tax return, shoplifting. This is gunrunning on an industrial scale. With 600 assault rifles, you could start a revolution in a third world country. Christ! You could start a revolution in this country!' The distant sound of a diesel engine brings our informative discussion to a halt. 'Oi, give me a leg-up,' I say. He cups his hands together and lifts me high enough to peer out between a crack in the eaves. 'Shit! That's all we need.'

'What? What is it?'

'Clarence has pulled up at the farmhouse.'

'Great! Let's get the lid back on this box and tie it up.'

'Hang on, two guys have walked out of the other hay shed and are now talking with Clarence.'

'What are they saying?'

I stare down at him. 'They're asking him if he can recommend a good French patisserie. How the fuck would I know what they're saying? We're over three hundred yards away! Whatever it is they're talking about, it doesn't appear too friendly. It's safe to assume it's not a school reunion. Sweet jizzcock!'

'I don't like the sound of that,' Geordie says, slightly alarmed.

'Do you want the good news or the bad news?'

'After the day I've had, give me the good news first.'

'You remember that signed Bob Dylan T-shirt I thought I'd lost?'

'What about it?'

'I found it last week. It had slipped down the back of my sock drawer.'

'Congratulations! I've been unable to sleep for weeks worrying about that. And the bad news?'

'The three of them have jumped into the truck and they're heading our way.'

'Crap and shite!' he yells as he pulls his hands away. I land with a thud on top of the crates and collapse in a crumpled heap. 'Well done, Bill! Thanks to your busybody meddling you've navigated us right up shitters ditch!' he hisses as we put the lid back on the crate and stamp at it with our feet, hoping the nails will catch. The lid won't comply and sticks out awkwardly.

'Hell, that stands out like the dog's nuts. I have an idea. You lift one up from below and we'll drop the opened one into its space and place the good one on top.'

'Good thinking, Bill.' The crate weighs a ton, but Geordie eventually heaves one up and we swap bales. 'Come on, let's get out of here,' he says.

'Hang on. Lift me up again. It may be too late.' I peer out through the eaves. 'Okay, let me down.'

'Well?'

'No chance. They're halfway up the track with an unhindered view of the barn.'

'So what? We'll casually saunter out and I'll explain that I came for my lost phone.' I think for a moment as my heart raps on my chest.

'That might work if it was Clarence by himself. But we don't know the other two from a loaf of bread. I bet you a penny to a pound of shit they're the two geezers I saw last night. They weren't heading to Flexley; they were heading to the farm.'

'What's the worst they can do?' the oaf replies.

'Erm… kill us after first torturing us to find out what we know.'

'Don't talk wet! You're letting your imagination run riot.'

'Is that right? How much do you think this little lot is worth?' I say, pointing at the crates.

'I couldn't say, exactly. I suppose an assault rifle may be around £1500 to £2000.'

'That's if it's bought legitimately, which may I remind you, is against the law in this country. On the black-market, and smuggled through many countries, you could double or triple that price. We're sitting on top of millions. People who smuggle guns worth millions aren't the sort of characters who are going to buy the "oh, I lost my phone" story.'

He appears thoughtful. 'Aye, perhaps you're right. What's the plan then?' That's a damn good question.

'The plan?'

'Aye, you're always the man with a plan.'

'Here's a novel idea for you... why don't you come up with a plan for a change?' He appears baffled, as though I've asked him to solve time travel. As I gaze around the barn, I notice the roller door slightly ajar. 'I'll tell you what the plan is...' His face brightens. 'You get down off these bales and close the barn door... slowly. Then get back up here. We'll lie down at the back and wait until they've gone. Then we'll leg it.'

His face darkens. 'I've got to say, out of all the plans you've ever come up with, this is not one of your better ones.'

'Shut up! You're wasting time.' He swiftly climbs down, grumbling as he does so.

'Aye, you leave it to muggins here to do the dirty work, even though it's you that got us into this unholy mess.' He darts across the barn and slams the roller door shut. *Christ! Give me strength!*

'I said to close it slowly, you cock!'

191

'I forgot,' he says as he dashes across the barn and scrambles back up.

'Great. If they saw the door being slammed shut like that, then we're as good as fucked!'

'Stop your blether, man. The truck was a way off.'

'Damn and blast! I've left my backpack in the corner near the door.'

'I'm beginning to think you're a Jonah. Well, you can bloody get it. It seems to me, I'm the only one doing any work around here.' I hear the truck come to a halt outside.

'Too late. Let's hope Clarence doesn't notice it.'

We crawl to the back of the bales and lie down. The roller door screeches and whines as it's pushed open. I've got to admit it, I'm cacking my undies. The truck rumbles in. A few seconds later, the engine dies as doors open, then slam shut.

'I'm very disappointed in you, Scimitar,' Clarence booms, trying to rein in his anger. 'The entire operation may have been put in jeopardy, due to your amateurish actions. You're experienced, you know the procedures, the rules. You don't come ashore until you see the signal and you *never ever* rendezvous at the farm!' he yells.

'Don't raise your voice to me, old man,' snarls a middle eastern voice. 'We are here because we saw the signal last night—two red parachute flares—the sign for us to come ashore.' I glance at Geordie, who offers an apologetic cringe.

'I'm telling you; I didn't send any flares up last night, not with the storm brewing. It would have been too dangerous.'

'Then who let the flares off?'

'I don't know. I've heard nothing on the grapevine about a boat being in trouble. Probably kids. Bloody idiots!' I edge forward and stare down at them. They're all standing, facing each other, near the barn door. Their body language is aggressive. I feel Geordie inch along beside me. Clarence rubs at his chin as though deep in thought.

'It's a good job I allowed a two-day window to do the exchange,' he mutters,' as if to himself.

'We were nearly seen,' adds the guy with the middle eastern accent.

'What do you mean?' Clarence whispers suspiciously.

'What do you call them? Your bloody English marine rescue vessel was heading our way. Luckily, we made it to the cove in time and waited there for a good three hours until we were sure they had gone.'

'The cove is only ten minutes away. You should have made it there before the lifeboat was even in the water.'

'The engine went kaput, and we had to row.'

'Jesus, what a bloody balls up from start to finish,' Clarence barks. The guy who has remained silent is a mean-looking bugger. Shaven headed with tattoos on his neck. He's short and stocky, ripped muscles. Definitely ex-services. Clarence emits a long sigh as he rubs his hand over his bald nut. 'It is what it is. I guess there's no harm done.' He looks at the stocky man. 'Has your partner got a name?'

'He's called "The Cossack". That's all you need to know.'

'That's all I want to know. Let's get down to business.'

'You have our merchandise?' Scimitar asks. Clarence spins around and holds his arm out towards the hay bales. We drop our heads.

'Hidden in those bales. 660 AK-47s and a million rounds of ammunition, as agreed. I've already moved one load.'

'And our transport?'

'Waiting, moored up on the river. Two sea barges to take you across to Ireland. Once there, you'll hunker down for a night before the guns are transferred to a fishing trawler which will sail to the drop off point at the Port of Benghazi.'

'Very good work, Clarence,' Scimitar says, with an accompanying smile. Clarence appears impatient.

'What about my merchandise? I take it they're in your backpack?' The Cossack says something to Scimitar, and they engage in a few minutes' discussion in Russian.

'First… we see the guns,' Scimitar says, nodding at the bales. *Shit!*

'No! I want to inspect my goods to make sure they're the real deal,' Clarence demands.

'No. Guns first,' Scimitar replies, standing his ground.

'Listen to me, you little wop bastard, you're on my patch now, you follow my rules!' Clarence explodes as he lurches towards Scimitar. In a lightning-quick move, The Cossack pulls a small pistol out from the back of his pants and plants it firmly on Clarence's temple.

'Halt!' he yells. My buttocks involuntarily clench. Clarence's demeanour changes... funny about that. Conciliatory gestures replace bellicose behaviour.

'Now, now, boys, take it easy. No need for that. Put the gun away and let's talk,' Clarence smiles benevolently at them. Scimitar nods at The Cossack, who lowers the gun. 'Fine, we'll look at the guns.' Scimitar makes his way to the bales and starts to climb.

'Nice plan, Bill,' Geordie whispers, as we wait for the inevitable. 'What now?'

'We'll take him hostage.'

'With what exactly?' I fumble in my pocket and pull out my micro-penknife.

'With this,' I say as I hand it to him. Geordie's eyes widen in disbelief.

'And what am I supposed to do with this?' he asks as he prises open the one-inch blade.

'Hold it to his throat.'

'Oh, aye, I could give him a nasty nick with this. Either that or cut his toenails for him. Did you get this in a Christmas cracker?'

'It's all we have. He won't know the size of it.' We feel the hay bales rock as Scimitar begins to scale them. A hand materialises a few feet from us followed by a shock of curly black hair.

17: The Booty

'Wait!' Clarence yells. 'Scimitar, come down. I'll start the forklift and drop a pallet onto the back of the truck.' Scimitar's hand vanishes. The throaty roar of the forklift starts up, sending diesel fumes into the air.

'Christ, that was close,' Geordie mutters. We edge our way back into the furthest recesses. The hydraulics of the forklift whine into action. A moment later, a pallet of bales is removed not too far from where we are lying, spreadeagled. We wait until we hear the clank of the pallet hitting the bed of the truck, then edge forward again. The Cossack jumps up, pulls a large hunting knife from a sheath on his belt, slices the twine, then feeds the blade into the edge of the lid. One expert twist and the cover pops off.

'Now that's what you call a knife,' Geordie murmurs. The Cossack pulls out a rifle and throws it down to Scimitar who runs his eye over it.

'Happy now?' Clarence quizzes. Scimitar passes the rifle back to The Cossack, who drops it into the crate and reattaches the cover with a lot more skill and ease than our attempt. Scimitar nods at Clarence, removes his backpack and hands it to him. Clarence carefully opens the bag and extracts two parcels wrapped in bubble wrap. He shakes his head in contempt.

'Bloody amateurs,' he snaps. 'These should have been transported in specially designed shockproof containers.' His anger subsides as excitement and awe overwhelm him. He carefully undoes the wrapping on one parcel and holds a purple, bejewelled egg in front of him. I think he's about to burst into tears. 'Oh, the beauty, the elegance. Sheer magnificence! A work of art,' he gushes as he leans forward and kisses the egg, tenderly. He repeats the process with the next parcel. The second egg is verdant green, streaked with gold netting, resting on a gold pedestal. He wipes a tear from his eye.

'What the hell are those,' Geordie says under his breath. 'Glorified Easter eggs?'

'They're Faberge.'

'What... chocolate Easter eggs?'

'Will you shut the fuck up!' I hiss in his ear. Clarence gently wraps the eggs in the bubble wrap and places them carefully in the bag. Geordie nudges me in the ribs.

'Bill, I've got a fart coming,' he whispers.

'Hold it in,' I say through gritted teeth.

'I'm not sure I can. It's one of those wilful little bastards with a mind of its own.'

'I didn't realise flatus had personalities.'

'This one has. It's the stealth fart. A malevolent little bugger, and it feels like a wet one. I could end up spray-painting my undies. It's going to bust the doors wide open whether I like it or not.' I get a sudden flashback to my peaceful bedroom in the Yorkshire Dales and my conversation with Fiona. "Camping will be fun." Her words reverberate around my head. Here I am, hiding on top of 600 AK-47s and a million rounds of ammo in a barn in Somerset. Below me is an ageing and ruthless gun runner and two cutthroat mercenaries, and international jewel thieves to boot. The cherry on top of the cake… a six-and-a-half-foot Scottish knucklehead, lying next to me, who cannot control his flatulence release.

'Geordie, I'm warning you! I know the decibels of your farts. They're the equivalent of a sonic boom. If you let one go now, guess what Clarence's pigs will be having for dinner tonight?'

'I'm sorry, Bill, but I cannae keep it in.' It starts slowly. A soft, high-pitched whistle that sounds like a balloon with a leak. It traverses up and down the mixolydian scale, twice, with a certain touch of elegance. There's something familiar about it, almost Beatlesque. It reminds me of a Paul McCartney song, but for the life of me, I can't remember which one. It reaches a crescendo on a dissonant note before diminishing to a natural resolution in the key of A minor. It's the best thing he's ever written. We both slide and wriggle away from the edge of the bales. I can no longer see faces, but I can hear voices.

'What was that?' Scimitar asks with alarm.

'I'm not sure,' Clarence begins. 'For a moment it sounded like the cry of a long-eared owl that's been on the piss. But they're rare around these parts, and they're nocturnal. Maybe I've got one nesting in the rafters.' There's confusion in his mind, but not suspicion. A few seconds of silence pass as I pray to God the Sasquatch doesn't release a thunderbolt. To make matters worse, his fart stinks. I feel quite giddy, amongst other things. The talking continues below but I'm concerned with a more pressing matter—asphyxiation.

'What is that odour?' Scimitar asks. Someone takes two hearty sniffs.

'Hmm… the wind must have changed direction. It's either the pigs or the silage pit may have filled with water after last night's storm.' Slowly, the stench abates as I attempt to breathe again. Someone blows their nose. I wish I could.

'Christ! That's ripe,' Geordie notes. I'm not willing to open my mouth to respond.

'What is the plan?' Scimitar inquires.

'We'll load the truck up with the guns and wait until dusk,' Clarence explains. 'You and The Cossack will then ride in the back of the truck, hidden by the hay bales. We drive down to the river, and on my say so, you both climb aboard a barge, go to the berth, and keep out of sight. My men will help unload the guns. I will make a further two trips until we have all the guns aboard. At dawn, tomorrow, the barges will set sail for Ireland. Until then, you both need to stay here, out of sight.'

'No, no, no,' Scimitar says, angrily. 'We are tired, dirty, hungry, and thirsty. We have not eaten or drunk anything in over fourteen hours.' Clarence eyes them up and down.

'Very well, climb into the back of the truck and keep your heads down. I'll take you back to the farmhouse. You can get showered and freshen up. I'll make a hot meal for you and provide refreshments. But after that, you need to come back to this barn. You can get some shuteye here for a few hours, out of the way. Agreed?'

'Agreed,' Scimitar says.

The truck pulls out of the shed and stops. The roller doors slam shut, and the truck takes off again. We wait five minutes until we can no longer hear the truck's engine, then clamber down from our perch, grab the backpack, and exit the barn. We need to cross the farm track to a stone wall ahead of us. In doing so, we'll be in full view of the farmhouse but there's no other option.

'Geordie, we need to jump the wall then we'll be out of sight. After three; one, two, three.' We scamper across the track and leapfrog the wall landing quietly in the field below.

*****

We set off at a good pace following our footsteps back to the campground.

'I tell you what, Bill.' Geordie begins.

'What?'

'Flaky was right about you.'

'In what way?' I ask, puzzled.

'You have an uncanny knack of always leading us into trouble.' I stop walking and take a gulp of water, glaring at him.

'I beg your pardon!' I exclaim.

'No point denying it. Your track record speaks for itself. You're a trouble-finder.'

'Excuse me! Let's look at some facts, shall we? Which dickhead let the flares off? Who was the knobjockey who incapacitated Clarence's farmhands and volunteered our services to help him move his bloody hay bales? Which tightarse picked the campsite solely because it was cheap? And lastly, who were the two wank merchants who said they were really keen to go camping in the first place?' He scratches at his chin, thoughtfully.

'Hang on a minute—I never wanted to go camping. I only agreed because Jackie said you and Robbo were nuts on the idea.'

I grin at him. 'Is that right. That's exactly what Fiona said to me about you and Robbo. We've been hoodwinked.'

'Those bloody women! The duplicitous, deceitful, devils. This is all their fault. Anyway, never mind about all that. What are we going to do about the guns? As much as it pains me to say it, we'll have to go to the police.' I slap him hard on the chest.

'Are you crazy!' I yell at him. 'What if Clarence has someone working on the inside? They'll feed us into a woodchipper faster than you can say Easter Bunny.'

'We cannae let 600 assault rifles and a million rounds of ammo be smuggled out of the country. Have you no conscience?'

'Oh, yes, I have a conscience, and two arms and two legs and a perfectly good head… and I want to keep all of them. We're dealing with terrorists and mercenaries. They snatched two Faberge eggs, worth millions, from under the noses of the Russians. What do you think they'll do to us, and possibly our families if we are the ones to ruin their little game?'

'What about an anonymous tip-off?'

'Nah… too risky.'

'So, what's the plan?'

'We go back to the campground, pack up our gear, and head off home straight away the girls return from their jolly day out.'

'They're not going to be happy about that.'

'No, they're not. But they're not going to be over the moon when they find out their husbands have been turned into meat paste.'

'Come on, Bill, we've been in sticky situations before, and we've come out the other side. Remember the London gangsters?'

'Yes… the Finks. I remember them only too well. You took a bullet to the shoulder.'

'Aye, that's right. Not that I like to talk about it. Although, it does still give me merry hell when it's cold weather. It could affect my strumming arm in years to come. Another two inches to the right and it would have hit me clean in the heart.'

'I thought you didn't like to talk about it. Anyway, this is way different, Geordie. London gangsters dealing in drugs, stand-over protection money and knocked off gear is not the same as ideologically motivated terrorists—or freedom fighters, depending on your point of view. We are way out of our depth. The best plan.... the only plan, is to feign ignorance. Which, in your case, shouldn't be too much of an ask.'

'Okay, have it your way—but it doesn't sit well with me. Those rifles could end up taking thousands of innocent lives, including women and children.'

I understand this and the thought sickens me. 'We can't unscramble the egg, Geordie.'

'What the hell does that mean?'

'We can't turn back time. What's happened has happened and we can't change it. We know what we know. But we can still pretend we've seen and heard nothing. It's the safest option, for all of us.'

'Jesus, Bill, I hope you're right. I'm trusting you on this one. I couldn't live with myself if I find out those weapons end up killing wee ones.'

'No, nor me. There's nothing as precious as the innocent. It's a risk we're going to have to take.' I'm in an impossible situation. What am I supposed to do? Save the lives of people I've never met... or protect the ones I love. There's only one answer.

He drops to his haunches and picks at a blade of grass. 'Christ, what's happened to us, Bill?' His voice is soft, reflective. 'Once upon a time we wouldn't have thought twice about doing the right thing and dobbing on Clarence. Hell, we may have even cut out the middleman and set fire to the bloody shed, ourselves.' I kneel at his side and wrap my arm over his shoulder.

'I know. Those were the days when we knew no fear. That all changed the moment we had children. It's no longer about what's right and wrong, it's about the safety of our kids. That is paramount. Everything else comes a distant second. We can't change the world.'

'When I first met you, you believed that music could change the world, that's why you formed the band. When did it all change?' I stand up and let out a deep sigh.

'I'm not sure. It wasn't a sudden realisation that smacked me in the face one day. It's the nature of life.'

'What do you mean?'

'I remember the last time I ever saw my dad. He was in hospital, dying… he knew he didn't have long left.'

'I remember you saying. Wasn't it brain cancer?'

'No. A brain tumour. I asked him a stupid, thoughtless question. I asked him if he was scared of dying. He laughed and said dying was easy, it's living that's hard. I didn't understand what he meant at the time, but I do now. Living is a bloody tough gig, it's unrelenting. It kicks you in the guts every day. When you're eighteen and full of ideals and passion, you can soak up the punches. After twenty years of getting belted, you get weary. It's not about me or what I want anymore. It's about Mary and always will be… until life stops belting me. So, to answer your question; I don't know when I stopped believing music could change the world.'

203

'What's the point of it then? What's the point of us, of our band?'

'We're here to capture a moment in time. A shoulder to cry on during dark nights. We're the backing track when two people fall in love and share a kiss. We're the little boy who points at the emperor and laughs because he's not got any clothes on. That's what the point is. We can't change the world, but we can make someone's world seem a little better. Hey, I've had a great idea for our next album,' I say trying to lift the mood and change the subject simultaneously.

'What?' he mumbles without much interest.

'A dance album.' He rubs at his eyes with the back of his hand and stands up.

'Have you had a bang to the head?'

'I'm serious. I'm thinking of something trippy with heavy rhythms and some seriously cool bass lines. A happy album that makes people get up and dance. When was the last time you danced?'

'I dunno. Did I dance at my last birthday?'

'I'm not sure it could be called dancing. You looked like someone had stuck a firecracker up your arse.'

He laughs. 'Aye, well, I hit the whisky a little early on that particular night.'

'Come on, let's dance.'

'Don't talk bloody daft!' I grab his arms and begin singing "The Last Waltz" by Engelbert Humperdinck. 'Give over you silly bugger!' he yells, mortified, as I spin him around. I stare, romantically, into his eyes. He puts up resistance for a few seconds until he succumbs to my charms and joins me in the verse and chorus. As we finish the finale, we collapse in a heap on the grass and roll around laughing.

'We'll be right, Bill. We always get out the other side… one way or another,' he chuckles. For once, I hope he's right.

'Come on, big fella, let's get back. We can't leave the Dynamic Duds in charge for too long.'

18: The Missing

As we stroll down the hill towards our camp, it's not a reassuring sight.

'Look at those two wankers,' Geordie says. Robbo is lying flat out on a picnic blanket, snoring, and Flaky is sitting in the same chair as we left him over three hours ago. His head droops back so far over the headrest that the front legs tilt slightly off the ground. He's snoring, softly. Geordie saunters up to Robbo and jabs the toe of his trainer into his ribs.

'What the!' Robbo's sweet dreams end abruptly. He stares up at Geordie through dark sunglasses. 'Hey man… that's totally uncool. I was catching a few Zs.'

'Is that right? You're lucky you didn't catch a punch up the throat. We left you two bollock brains in charge of the laddies and lassies.'

'Chill man, no need to go on a downer. The kids are fine. They're in Will's campervan playing shops.' Geordie marches up to Flaky, sticks the toe of his trainer under the chair leg and jerks it upwards. Flaky catapults backwards. He lands on his head and does a reverse somersault. He's momentarily confounded, as one would be.

'Where am I? What day is it?' he whines as he staggers to his feet, unaware that Geordie had anything to do with his downfall.

'Asleep on duty! If this were a war, you'd be facing a firing squad at dawn.'

'What the hell are you gibbering about?' Flaky replies as he rights his chair and falls into it. I open the camper door and poke my head inside. The girls are all busy with various tins and packets of food, lined neatly up on the table. Sally is the shopkeeper, while Mary and Katrina are the shoppers. The boys are noticeable by their absence.

'Hi, girls,' I say. 'Where are Wallace and Robert?' Sally and Katrina shrug as they barter over a can of baked beans. 'Mary?' She appears distracted as she counts her pretend money. 'Mary, where are the boys?' She looks up at me.

'They got bored of playing shops and said they were going on an adventure.' The alarm bells immediately ring.

'What sort of adventure?' I quiz in a sterner voice which makes her stop counting her money.

'I don't know.' I jump off the step and turn to my mates.

'Flaky, when was the last time you saw Wallace and Robert?' I demand. He raises his head, painfully.

'About thirty minutes ago. They were in the van. Aren't they there?'

'No!'

'I definitely didn't see them leave.'

'You wouldn't, would you! Too busy in the land of nod!' Geordie bellows.

'Shite! Mary said they were talking about going on an adventure!' Geordie runs towards his tent shouting their names, over and over as I frantically rush from van to van. Robbo and Flaky circumnavigate the motorhomes peering underneath, also calling out to them. Geordie returns from the tent.

'They're not there. Wait until I get my hands on them. They know they're not supposed to wander off. Where the hell can they be? Jackie will crucify me when she finds out.'

'Calm down, you're not ⸺helping the situation,' I advise. 'They can't have gone too far in thirty minutes.' I head back to the campervan to question the girls again.

'Sally, Mary, Katrina, this is very, very important. Are the boys hiding somewhere to give us a fright? If they are, you need to tell us, as it's very serious. I promise no one will be in trouble, but you must tell the truth.' They all appear upset and go silent. 'Well?' I yell, making them wince. They all shake their heads vigorously.

'No, daddy. They're not hiding. I told you they were going on an adventure.'

'What sort of adventure?'

'Rock climbing. But they told us not to tell you.' I leap from the van.

'What is it?' Geordie asks with a tormented expression.

'They were going on a rock climbing adventure.' We all instinctively turn towards the cliff in the distance. Fear holds us in its icy grip. 'Geordie, you come with me, we'll check out the cliffs. Robbo, you head up to the main road and make sure they're not up there. Flaky, you stay here and mind the kids. Ring the police and tell them we have two missing children.'

'Are you sure we can trust him with that simple task?' Geordie says, glaring at him. Flaky appears to be on the edge of a nervous breakdown.

'Leave it out, Geordie! It could have happened to any of us. Have you never nodded off when left in charge? Come on, we're wasting time!' We set off at a steady jog downhill. We slide through the wire fence and stand on the path, panting hard. 'We better split up,' I say, staring up and down the coastal track. 'I'll head south towards the river—you go north towards Flexley. Keep your phone handy and call me as soon as you see anything.'

'Oh, tatties over the side,' he murmurs, his eyes full of sorrow.

'What's wrong?'

'My phone's dead. I cannae think straight, Bill. My head's mince.' I slap him hard on the back.

'Oi! Buck up your ideas. Now's not the time to go all weak on me. We're going to find those lads... alive and well. Do you hear me?' He raises his head and nods.

'Aye, you're right. I'll yell out if I see anything.' We both turn to go our separate ways when a weak, distant trill carries to us on the blustery wind.

'Wait! Did you hear that?' I've already set off running along the cliff towards the river. I'm exhausted, dehydrated and feeling lightheaded but the adrenalin is like a drug fuelling my legs. Geordie is now by my side. After about 200 yards, we spot a tiny figure in the distance waving at us.

'That looks like one of them.'

'That's Robert, I swear to God! He was wearing that bright red T-shirt this morning.' Geordie shouts his name and waves. Robert waves back. We increase our pace much to the anguish of my burning lungs. Within thirty seconds we reach Robert. His tear-stained face doesn't bode well. Geordie gathers him up in one giant arm.

'Where's your brother?' he demands. Robert points over the cliff. I lie down near the edge and carefully crawl forward until my head is staring at the enormous drop to the frothy waters below. I glance to my left and spot Wallace about seven or eight feet from the top. He's standing on a narrow stone ledge with his arms spread out against the rock face, frigid with fear. It's a precarious position, but at least the ledge is holding him safe for the moment.

'Wallace!' I shout. He gingerly gazes upwards. 'Keep calm. Me and your dad will soon have you back up here.'

'Oh no!' he wails. 'My da's gonna do his nut. I'm in big trouble.'

'Wallace, you're not in trouble. I'm just glad you're safe,' Geordie yells as he sticks his melon over the brink and gazes down on his son.

'I wouldnae call this bloody safe,' Wallace moans. I turn to Geordie.

'The lad's got a sense of humour.'

'I'm scared,' Wallace cries, tearing up.

'It's all right to be scared, son. Everyone gets scared sometimes.'

'You're never scared.'

'That's not true. I get scared by a lot of things.'

'What are you scared of?'

'Ghosts and people with large ears. They give me the creeps.'

Wallace chuckles 'There's no such thing as ghosts,' he stammers.

'You're right. So how silly is that? Being scared of something that doesn't exist. It's all in my mind. That's what fear can do... it can play tricks on you. Guess what happens when fear comes up against brave, though?'

'What?'

'Brave always wins because it's tougher and stronger. I want you to be brave. Can you do that for me?'

'Aye,' says Wallace as a ripple of reassurance spreads across his face. I'm baffled by how he ended up in such a spot. It's almost a sheer drop. There are barely any footholds or anything to cling to.

'Right, I'm coming to get you. Your Uncle Bill is going to lower me over the edge by my feet.' It's bloody news to me! 'I'll reach out to you, then you're going to have to grab my hands. Do you understand?'

'What if you drop me?'

'Listen, son, once I have hold of you there's no way I'll drop you... promise.'

'You might not drop Wallace, but there's no guarantee I won't drop you,' I say. 'I don't think I can hold your weight. We'll do it the other way around. You hold me and I'll go over the edge.' He stares at me for a second.

'Aye, okay,' he says rather too quickly for my liking.

'Don't hold me by the pants or shoes, grab me on the bare skin above the ankles.' He stands behind me and takes hold of my legs. I use my hands to walk forward. As I reach the edge and stare down, I'm overcome with fear. 'Hang on a second. I'm experiencing a panic attack.' My breathing is erratic, and my heartbeat is performing a punk rock drum roll. I try not to fight or reason with the anxiety. After twenty seconds it subsides. I feel calm, grounded, confident.

'You ready, Bill?'

'Yep, let's do it!' I drop over the lip and paw my way down the cliff face, inch by inch. As I get about two feet away from Wallace, I experience another unwelcome sensation; I'm now dangling. The only thing between me and death is Geordie's grip. 'Another foot or so,' I call out.

'No can do, Bill. I'm right on the edge. I cannae go any further otherwise the two of us will be taking a bath,' he replies.

'Can you sit or kneel?'

'It's difficult to do whilst holding your legs. I'll try to squat.' I drop a little further until I'm nearly within the grasp of Wallace yet still tantalisingly out of reach. He makes a sudden grab for me and nearly slips off the ledge.

'No!' I shout, alarming the boy. I need to speak calmly to him. He's visibly shaking. 'Wallace, I don't want you to move. You don't need to do anything until I say so. Geordie, a bit more.'

'I'm at my limit, Bill, and I'm getting tired. I'm pulling you back up.' He drags me up and I lie on my back panting and staring up at the sky. A seagull is riding the thermals, swooping, and soaring like a kite. I'm not sure what its purpose is… if any. Maybe it does it for fun. Do seagulls do things for fun? The sobs of Robert refocus my thoughts.

'Da, is Wallace going to die?' he sniffles.

'No, he's not, son. Me and Uncle Billy will save him. Just you see.' I jump to my feet and squint back towards the campsite. There's activity as a police car makes its way down the hill.

'The cavalry's here.' Geordie has a quick glance over his shoulder.

'I cannae wait for them. I'm going down to get my lad.'

'Don't be stupid! You'll both end up...' I stop myself.

'What...dead? Do you think I'm going to stand here twiddling my thumbs while my son is clinging to the edge of that bloody rock?'

'Geordie, I know you're emotional but you're not being logical. The cops will be here in a minute.'

'And what are they going to bloody do?'

'I don't know. Maybe, they've contacted air-sea rescue or something.' He's already at the cliff edge perusing his options.

'That ledge is only about eight feet down. If you hold my hands, I can lower myself onto it.'

'And then what?'

'I'll lift him up onto my shoulders and you grab him.'

'And how are you going to get back up?'

'We'll cross that bridge when we come to it.'

'Just wait for the bloody police!'

'If that were Mary down there, what would you do?' There's no reasoning with him. He's already turned his back to the sea and dropped to his knees as he lowers himself over the edge. I kneel and grab his giant hands. He stares at me. 'Good man,' he smiles. 'Bill, if anything should happen to me, then you'll take care of Jackie and the boys, won't you? I mean financially and all that. I can't bear to think of them struggling.'

'Nah… I'll get Jackie on the game and sell your lads on the internet. You daft twat! Anyway, you better get your arse back up here because we've still got four songs to finish for the new album. I can't do it without you.'

'Aye, that's true. Righto, here I go. Hang on, Wallace… I'm coming.' I lean back as I take his weight, which is considerable. I hear voices and glance along the path. Two figures are running towards us. 'Bill, another inch or two and I'm there.' I lean forward slightly and get a dizzy rush to the head as I gaze at the crashing waves below. As he makes purchase with the rock, the tension in my arms is released and I let go of his hands.

'Will! Will!' Flaky shouts as he nears. He's followed, some distance behind, by a police officer. Flaky grabs Robert and gives him a hug. 'Oh, you're safe, thank God! Where's your brother?' Robert points at the cliff. 'Oh, no.' Flaky peers over and sways. 'Jeepers creepers,' he whispers. The copper arrives on the scene. It's our old friend, Sergeant Waygood.

'What's the situation?' he says, panting hard.

'Young lad, about eight feet down, on a narrow ledge. His father has just joined him.' The sergeant lies down on the grass and peeks over.

'Bloody fool,' he murmurs. 'I'll call air-sea rescue. We can winch them out of there.'

'Bill, I'm going to lift Wallace onto my shoulders.'

'Geordie, stay where you are. Air-sea rescue will be here soon.'

'Don't be stupid! The downdraft will blow us to kingdom come!' I glance at Sergeant Waygood.

'He has a point. Hey, where's Robbo?' I ask Flaky.

'I haven't seen him. I guess he's still checking the road.'

'Who the hell is looking after the girls?' I shout glaring at him.

'Calm down. Twitchy is back.'

'Oh, I see. Why don't you take Robert back to the camp, you know, just in case.'

'In case what?' the halfwit replies.

'Use your imagination,' I snap. He appears stumped for a moment until the penny drops.

'Oh, yes. Of course. Robert, come with me and we'll get a drink of lemonade.'

'I want to stay here,' the boy wails.

'Robert!' I yell at him. 'Go with your Uncle Flaky, right now!' It's the first time I've ever raised my voice to the lad, and he looks terrified. Flaky leads him away. 'Flaky, hang on, I've had a thought. In the back of Twitchy's car is a rope. I spotted it the other day when he gave us a lift back from…' I pause and re-evaluate my words before I utter them.

'A lift back from?'

'From… erm… never mind that now! Get back to the camp as fast as you can and tell him to get his arse down here with the rope.'

'Come on Robert, we need to run.' Sergeant Waygood is on his radio requesting backup. I hold my breath as Geordie picks Wallace up and lifts him onto his shoulders. The problem is, Wallace is bent almost double, clinging desperately to Geordie's hands.

'Wallace, let go of my hands, otherwise, Uncle Will cannae reach you.'

'But I'm scared, dad.'

'I know. Remember what I said? Be brave and brave will win. It always does. I've got hold of your feet. You can't fall.' The lad is shaking like a shitting dog. One misstep now and both will plummet a hundred feet to the rocks below.

'Wallace, let go of your dad's hands and stand upright.'

'Easy for you to say, Uncle Billy.' Yep, he's definitely developed a warped sense of humour. He lets go of Geordie and thrusts his arms out to his side for balance.

'That's the way,' I whisper. 'Nice and easy. Right, lift your arms above your head and me and Sergeant Waygood will grab you.' As his body unfurls to its full height, he raises his arms over his head. I nod at the Sergeant.

'Okay,' he replies. We gently grab him by the wrists and pull him up onto the soft grass. I give him a big hug.

'Wallace, I want you to run back to the camp and bring a bottle of water for your dad.'

216

'Okay, Uncle Bill. I'm a fast runner,' the boy replies with a grin.

'Hell, and thunder,' Sergeant Waygood complains as he flops onto his back. 'I'm getting too old for all this malarky.'

I smile at him. 'You'll be able to relax tonight with a couple of beers and tell yourself you helped save a young boy's life. There can't be many better feelings than that.'

'I suppose so.'

'He's safe, Geordie,' I shout as I peer over the cliff. For a split second, I'm completely bamboozled. I glance over my shoulder at Sergeant Waygood.

'What's wrong?' he asks, noticing my befuddlement.

'He's gone.'

19: The Calamity

A million thoughts siphon through my mind in a nanosecond. Jackie's distraught face; the tear-stained cheeks of Wallace and Robert; Fiona's questions of how this all came about; an unfinished album; the money he owed Robbo; a half-used toilet roll sitting on the camp table. It's strange what one thinks about in times of calamity.

'What do you mean, he's gone?'

'Look for yourself.' We both gawp at the empty ledge. I must have entered a state of shock because I feel nothing. No panic, no despair, no sorrow, no guilt. I'm a blank canvas, emotionless. The Sergeant and I both stare at each other for what feels like an eternity. His lips move, accompanied by facial expressions, but I hear nothing. My hearing has gone… I'm totally deaf. I float heavenwards and gaze down on the back of my head and the peaked cap of the Sergeant. It's the most serene thing I've ever experienced. I want it to last forever.

'Fuck me rigid! That was a bloody close call!' Geordie's voice booms up the cliff-side. My out-of-body experience comes to an explosive halt as reality hits me in the head like a wrecking ball and I re-enter my physical body. Suddenly, all my senses are very much alive and working overtime. Cortisone fires through my nerves and synapses. The roar of the sea and the screech of seagulls deafen me. I hear voices and turn to see Twitchy and Flaky, sprinting our way.

'Geordie! Where are you?'

'About twelve feet below where I used to be!' his voice echoes back.

'Are you okay?' the Sergeant calls out.

'Oh, aye! Never better. The views are grand from here.'

'State your position,' Sergeant Waygood cries.

'My what?'

'Your position.'

'My position? I think the technical term is—fucked!'

'No, I mean, are you on a shelf or ledge? Are you injured or incapacitated in any way?'

'I'm a bit bruised and I've grazed my knee. I have one foot stuck into a small crevice to take a bit of my weight, but mostly I'm keeping myself upright by clinging onto a small sapling which doesn't appear too pleased with proceedings.'

'What's below you?'

'Air! About a hundred feet of it.'

'Not good then?'

'I can see why you're a copper. Sharp as a tack!'

'Can you hang on for another ten minutes?'

'Well, I do have a basket of washing the missus told me to hang out... but I guess it can wait.' Sergeant Waygood shakes his head and purses his lips.

'Smart-arse, is he, your mate?'

'You're half-right. Geordie, don't worry, Twitchy is on his way,' I call down to him.

'It never rains but pours. Are you trying to finish me off?'

'He's got a rope.' I jump to my feet as Twitchy and Flaky arrive.

'Where is he?' Twitchy asks, panting but completely unruffled by events.

'Over there, below that small ledge, out of view. He's hanging onto a small tree. We've not got long, or rather, he hasn't.' Twitchy takes a peek.

'Ha! Piece of cake. He'll be back up here in a jiffy.' He throws his coat on the ground, ties the rope off to a fence post, then pulls cords and various rock climbing paraphernalia from his backpack.

'Are you a rock climber?'

'Yes. If you're serious about bird watching, you need to be.' He attaches various cords and metal clips to the rope. 'Right, a simple foot loop attached to a French Prusik knot and a klemheist knot above the Prusik should do the trick.'

'My thoughts exactly,' I say as he performs his dark arts with speed and dexterity. 'Is it safe? He's a big lad.'

'Safe? No of course it's not safe, it's fraught with danger. All rock climbing is. There are multiple fail points and to make it even more dangerous, I don't have a harness with me. Has your friend done any rock climbing before?'

'I've never heard him mention it. I'll check. Yo! Geordie! Have you ever done any rock climbing before?' I holler down to him.

'Aye, when I was at school. I was one of the best rock…'

'No, he hasn't,' I say, ignoring the buffoon. 'Treat him as an imbecile with limited intelligence and spell everything out to him in the simplest of layman's terms.'

'Billy Boy!'

'What?'

'This sapling…' he cries, followed by silence.

'What about it?'

'Its roots are coming out. I think this could be it. Tell Jackie and the boys I'll always be watching over them.'

'Geordie, just another minute or two and Twitchy will be with you.'

'Hey, Bill?'

'What?'

'Cheers.'

'For what?'

'For being the best pal, any man could ever wish for… despite you being a moody, taciturn, grumpy, old, bastard! I'll miss you, buddy! See you on the other side. I'll keep a cold one waiting for you!' I turn to Twitchy and yell at him.

'For God's sake, hurry up, man! We've only seconds left.'

He gives me a stern glare. 'I'm following due process. Rush things, and there could be two fatalities instead of one. Safety first.'

'There's no time! Just get down there!'

'I'm go… go… go…' Oh, sweet Lord. Not now, please! His jaw lurches forward with each syllable. 'Go… go… go…'

221

'Going?' I prompt.

'Yes. I'm go… go… go…'

'We've established you're going.'

'As fast as I can poss… poss… poss…'

'Possibly?'

'Yes.'

'You're going as fast as you possibly can?'

'Yes. I'm going as fast as I can poss… poss… possibly go without en… en… en…' This is like playing a parlour game in the bowels of hell with Satan controlling the countdown clock.

'What are you trying to say? Entering, entertaining, encouraging, entrusting, enquiring?'

'Whoa! She's coming away, Bill. This sapling has decided it's had enough.'

'En… en… endangering my own life.' I breathe a sigh of relief as he finally spits the words out. He tosses the line over the cliff, leans back, then abseils down. Within seconds, he's disappeared from view.

'Have you reached him?' I shout.

'Yes! He's safe… at least for the moment.' Sergeant Waygood walks away as he gives an update to his superiors via radio. I bend down to pick up Twitchy's jacket. A couple of bank cards spill from his pocket. I pick them up and go to place them back in his jacket… but stop. One is a Barclays Bank card. The other has a mugshot of Twitchy, a number and the heading "National Crime Agency".

Underneath is a title, "Field Operative" followed by the name, "Todd Grimes". Hmm... it appears Twitchy is not who he says he is.

A few minutes pass until Geordie's body comes into view. He stands tall in the rope, pushes one knot up, bends slightly at the knee and then pushes another knot up. It's a laborious and slow process. As he nears safety, Sergeant Waygood and I reach out and haul him onto the ground.

'Never a dull moment,' he murmurs as he lies on his back, panting, and sweating profusely. 'We really need to come camping more often. All this fresh air and adventure is good for the appetite.' Sergeant Waygood leans over him.

'Geordie, I need to do a quick inspection to make sure you've no serious injuries.'

'Aye, whatever,' he replies as Wallace comes running down the track with a bottle of water. I gather the rope and wind it into a coil.

'Twitchy! I'm about to throw the rope down, so watch out.' A voice to my left, some distance away, calls out.

'No need.' I turn to see Twitchy pull himself onto the top of the cliff. I walk over to him. 'There was a way back up, but I must admit, it was harder than it looked.' I hand him his jacket. 'Rock faces can be deceptive,' he says, smiling as he catches his breath.

'As can NCA operatives,' I reply as I pass him his ID card. He appears stunned. 'It fell out when you took your jacket off,' I explain. He takes the card and slips it into his back pocket.

'Under no circumstances must you divulge my identity to anyone. Do you understand? I'm undercover on a critical mission.'

I smile at him. 'This critical mission... it doesn't involve gun-running and two stolen Faberge eggs, does it?' His demeanour immediately changes. Gone is the harmless, slightly eccentric, bird watcher with a terrible stammer. The muscles tighten on his face. His eyes drill into mine.

'I've had you all checked out,' he whispers. 'You are who you say you are. A rock band on a family holiday together. What do you know about guns and Faberge eggs?'

'Quite a lot. Purely by accident, may I add. I'll tell you everything I know on one proviso.'

'Go on.'

'You own the information. You figured it all out yourself. I don't want my name, or any of my family and friends, mentioned.' He pulls a cigarette packet out of his jacket and offers me one, as he takes one himself. We spark up.

'The eggs,' he begins, 'were stolen from the Kremlin Armoury. You can imagine how sophisticated their security system is. Whoever stole them knew exactly what they were doing. The Russian's are embarrassed about it, that's why they've not gone public with the information. They want to retrieve the eggs as quickly and quietly as possible with the least amount of fuss.'

'They don't want egg on their face.'

'Ha ha, very good. They are offering a million-pound reward for any information which will lead to the safe return of the eggs. If I keep your name out of it, you forgo the reward. That's a lot of money.'

I take a draw on my ciggy. 'I don't care about the money. All I care about is the safety of my family and friends. If, and when, you catch the culprits, I dare say there'll be a lot of very pissed off people. And they're not the sort of people you'd invite around to your house for Sunday dinner. They'll try to find out what went wrong and who the snitcher was. If my name is anywhere on your records or database, then I'm a sitting duck… and so is anyone associated with me.'

He nods thoughtfully. 'Hmm… okay. You tell me what you know, and I'll give you my word I won't mention your name. I'll take all the credit. It could be good for my career,' he adds, laughing. 'Anyway, to be honest, we don't really care about a couple of bloody eggs. It's the guns we want and the people who organised it.' I'm placing a lot of trust in him, but Geordie was right, we can't let those weapons reach their intended destination.

'Okay, deal.' We shake hands.

'Where can we talk privately?'

'My campervan, over a couple of beers.'

'Perfect.'

20: The Reckoning

The boys are sitting opposite me, each cradling a beer, unhappily ruminating on an eventful day. A day in which we averted tragedy by the skin of our teeth. We experience no joy, no elation. We are bereft of any congratulatory feeling. There's no solace in the fact that in a couple of days time the gun-runners will be swooped upon as they transfer their illegal shipment from the barges to a fishing vessel on the southwest coast of Ireland. At exactly the same time, the door to Clarence's farmhouse will be smashed in by a bevvy of undercover NCA operatives. We've prevented 600 assault rifles from entering a war-torn country, but we nearly lost the lives of one child and a moron.

I take a sip of beer, but it doesn't taste the same anymore. You know life has changed forever when your favourite brew tastes like battery acid. I glance over at the children who are sitting in a circle in the middle of the field playing a game that has them in fits of hysterics. How is it kids seem to shrug things off without a care in the world? Or so it seems. Who knows the long-term ramifications of today? Robbo's phone pings. He stares at the message.

'Oh, oh! Incoming verbal missile attack—ETA—approximately ten minutes,' he says with trepidation.

'The girls?' I say. He nods.

'What are you going to tell them?' Flaky asks.

'Me! I don't think so, brother! The boys didn't disappear under my watch,' I exclaim.

'It's not just about the boys. What about Clarence, the guns, the Faberge eggs?' Flaky responds.

I let out a long sigh. 'Fine, I'll tell them about that. But not about the boys,' I compromise. 'Do you know what makes me really sad, though?' I receive blank stares. 'The fact the girls will have had such a wonderful day. They'll have been shopping, maybe had a massage, eaten at a lovely restaurant, had a few glasses of expensive wine. They'll be on top of the world. It's rare when they get a chance to let their hair down. And when we tell them the news, it's going to ruin their day.'

'Perhaps we shouldn't tell them anything at all,' Flaky says.

'No... there should be no secrets between a husband and wife.'

'Who's going to tell them about Wallace and Geordie?' Robbo asks, as all eyes fall upon the big man himself, who is forlornly staring at his empty beer bottle clutched in his big mitt. There's a moment's silence until he lifts his head and realises the implications.

'Oh, I see! Even though I'm the hero, it falls to muggins to break the bad news and take a shellacking?' He gets no response. 'Fine. So be it,' he snaps before calming down. 'Anyway, it's probably for the best. I'm good with words. I'm adept at diffusing volatile situations.'

'You're adept at creating volatile situations,' Robbo drawls.

'Hey! Listen to me, Rip Van Winkle, I wasn't the one who nodded off whilst in charge of the kiddies!'

'Take it easy, big man. I was only joking.'

227

'We're all equally to blame. If I hadn't been so bloody inquisitive, then none of this may have happened,' I say.

'Hey, I've got a question for you,' Robbo says, gazing at me. 'Twitchy, or whatever his real name is, did he really have a stammer or was that all part of the cover?'

'Part of the cover. He bloody nailed it. But he is a keen birdwatcher which is handy when you work as an undercover field operative.' We fall silent. I gaze out across the sea, then to the verdant fields, inland. It is a beautiful spot, but I want to go home, back to the luxury of my house and the safety of the Yorkshire Dales.

The distant strains of "Mamma Mia," blaring out of a car sound system, rouse us from our private thoughts. A barrage of frenetic horn beeps follows, indicating the imminent arrival of the girls. *Here we go. This should be fun.* They park up and exit the car. Gillian has been driving and is sober. The other three, Fiona, Jackie, and Julie are well hammered. They teeter and totter towards us, laughing and giggling. Julie is holding an empty bottle of champagne. The three of them each carry an empty wine glass.

'Hey boys,' cries Jackie, 'did you miss us? I hope all the children are still alive,' she guffaws. 'Hang on… let me count them. One, two, three, four, five! Yep, all there, present and correct.' More laughter from the women. They're so amusing.

'Oh, Will! We've had the best day,' Fiona gushes. 'It was so much fun. First, we headed to Bath and had breakfast at a really nice café on the way. Then we got a manicure,' she adds as she flashes her nails at me. 'Then we went to a spa and got a massage followed by lunch at a Michelin Star restaurant.'

'It was only a one star, but it was fabulous,' Julie adds, as she cracks open a bottle of chilled white wine and fills four glasses to the brim. 'Here you go, Gillian. Thanks so much for driving.'

'My pleasure,' she replies, graciously as Julie hands the drinks out.

'On the way back, we called in at Weston-Super-Mare. We visited a lovely little pub overlooking the beach,' Jackie adds as she takes a hefty quaff of wine. Fiona sidles up to me and runs her fingers through my hair. I know the signs... she's feeling fruity, and for once my libido has gone AWOL.

'We got chatted up by four Royal Navy sailors on shore leave. They were all in their late twenties. They invited us back to their hotel for drinks.' All four of them burst out laughing.

'That's lovely, dear,' I say, morosely.

'They were so clean, youthful and very witty. They had us in stitches,' Julie says, blushing slightly.

'Nice one,' Robbo mutters, staring glassy-eyed at his full bottle of beer.

'They wanted us to stay the night,' Gillian adds, giggling.

'It was very tempting,' Fiona adds.

'Really,' I mumble. 'That would have been nice for you, dear.' The girls stop their effusive chatter and stare at us.

'My God! What's wrong with you lot!' Jackie barks. 'Has someone died?'

'What is it the media call them?' Julie starts. 'The "bad boys of rock 'n' roll". They belong in a retirement home, not a rock 'n' roll band.' More cackles of laughter. I notice Wallace has disentangled himself from the other children and races back to the adults.

'Ma! Ma!'

'Ah, here comes my little soldier.' Jackie puts her wine down and holds her arms out as Wallace leaps into them and is spun around. 'And how has my little warrior been? Have you missed your mammy?'

'Not really. Well, maybe a little. But you won't guess what happened today?'

'No, what?'

'We were allowed whatever we wanted for breakfast. Then we painted giant eggs. I made a hand-grenade, a dinosaur egg and... oh, I forget now. Then we played on the beach and after that, we flew kites. But the best part was—I fell down the cliff and got stuck. I thought I was going to die. Then Uncle Will and da came and rescued me. Then dad got stuck and nearly died and had to be rescued by that boring man who talks about birds.' Jackie stops swinging him around and drops him onto the ground. Robert calls out to his older brother.

'Wallace! Come on, we're starting the game again!' Wallace turns on his heels and races back to the other kids. The women look like they've been slapped across the chops with a wet haddock. Jackie turns to Geordie.

'That boy has a wild imagination. Geordie, please tell me he was exaggerating about the cliff?'

'I think I'll make cocoa for the children,' Flaky says as he rises quickly from his chair. 'It's been a long day and they really should be in bed soon. It's a lengthy drive home tomorrow. We all need a good night's sleep.'

'Yep, good idea,' Robbo concurs as he also rises hastily from his seat. 'I'll round them all up and get them showered and into their jim-jams.' A first for Robbo. A contemptible sneer spreads across Geordie's face as he watches them leave.

'Geordie, I asked you a question!' Jackie barks.

'Will, what's been going on?' Fiona asks with a concerned expression. The head rub has stopped.

'Ahem,' Geordie coughs. 'Well... it's like this. It sort of all started... no, wait. Let me gather my thoughts.'

'I'm waiting,' Jackie utters in a low, deep growl.

'Actually, you know what? My belly's not feeling too good. I'm away to the latrine.' He jumps from his chair, marches across to the table, picks up the toilet roll and sticks it under his armpit, and sets off. 'I'll let Bill explain. He's better with words than me,' he calls out. *What a trio of weak-kneed, gutless wonders!* Four sets of eyes now focus on me. I stand up, light a cigarette, pour myself a generous glass of white and smash it back in one hit.

'Ahem...' I begin, imitating Geordie's well-tested introduction to unwelcome news. 'I suggest you all refill your glasses and take a seat. It's a rather lengthy tale.' I'm hit by a sudden flashback to this morning when I told the boys that today would be the longest day. I reckon it has about another hour to go before it bloody ends. 'Okay... here we go. You all know Farmer Clarence, well...'

*****

231

I'm watching the Sunrise as I sip on strong black coffee and puff away on a smoke. It's peaceful as no one else has yet stirred. The sound of a zipper breaks my trance. Geordie wanders around the corner and pours himself a brew.

'How did you go sleeping in the boys tent?'

He grimaces at me. 'Bent double most of the night and it was bloody cold. But at least I have a clear head for once.'

'That's good. You have a lot longer to drive than the rest of us. You need to be fresh. Hey, the offer still stands; you can break the journey by dossing at our house tonight if you want.'

'Thanks, but I think it's best if we get home. It's not going to be much fun though, an eight-hour drive in stony silence.'

'It will pass, sooner than you think. Right, I'm going to start packing up the motorhome. May as well set off early. We'll miss a bit of traffic.'

'Aye. I'll finish my coffee then make a start on the tent.' The others are soon awake and it's not long before everyone pitches in with the decampment. The women have faces like slapped arses and they've sent all the men to Coventry… not a great spot to visit at the best of times. It takes about fifteen minutes to pack up the motorhomes… not so Geordie's tent. The children are flying their kites for one last time as the women congregate around the Range Rover and talk in hushed tones. I'm helping the boys dismantle the North Korean Big Top.

'I've got to say that yesterday's escapade has put a severe strain on my marriage,' Flaky states, looking deeply concerned. We all stare at him.

'Christ, Flaky, what's happened?' I ask, troubled by his statement. He stops winding up guy ropes.

'As I got out of bed this morning, she called me...' He removes his glasses and rubs them on his shirt.

'Go on,' Geordie says. 'She called you, what?'

'She called me an arsehole,' he whispers softly.

'And?' Robbo asks. Flaky looks surprised.

'That's it!' I let out a sigh of relief as Robbo and Geordie huff their annoyance.

'Is that all? Is that the pinnacle of your domestic strife? Your missus called you an arsehole,' Geordie sniggers. Flaky appears wounded.

'Yes. She's never used language like that towards me before.'

'I cannae believe that. You're an insufferable prig. If I were your wife, I'd be throwing knives at you the moment you stepped out of bed.'

'How long will Fiona give you the silent treatment?' Robbo asks as he lights a skinny joint.

'Oh, about an hour. Then she'll slowly let the drawbridge down. She's not one to let things fester. You?'

'About two hours. Julie's a lot like Fiona. There's no point in having bad blood. It does no one any good. She'll give me one more blast before she emerges from the trenches carrying a flag of truce.'

'And Jackie?' I say, turning to Geordie who is on the grass trying to force a piece of the tent into a holdall that appears way too small to handle it.

'Christ! How come when you buy a tent, everything fits into the bags perfectly. Then, when you try to pack it away, the bastard tent has expanded to twice its original size, and the bag has shrunk by half. Why can't they make the bags bigger. Sorry, what did you say?'

'I was inquiring how long Jackie will give you the silent treatment.'

'Oh,' he replies as he rubs his shirt sleeve across his brow. 'About two weeks… give or take.'

We're nearly ready to leave. Fiona, Julie, and Gillian are sauntering down the field to where the kids are still flying their kites. Geordie, Robbo and Flaky are forcing the last pieces of the tent into bags, accompanied by much cursing. I spot Jackie packing things into the boot of the Range Rover. I sidle over.

'Need a hand?'

'No, I'm fine,' she says, curtly. I light a smoke.

'You can't lay the blame for what happened yesterday solely at Geordie's feet. We're all to blame in a way. Flaky and Robbo nodded off. I let my curiosity get the better of me. In fact, Geordie is the most innocent out of all of us.' She stops rearranging things in the boot and fixes me with a fierce glare.

'Really… is that so? You always defend him, don't you? It was my precious boys who wandered off and their father wasn't there to keep an eye on them. They're not Robbo or Flaky's responsibility. They're Geordie's.'

'He only wanted to go to the farm to look for his phone. It was my idea we walked. We'd have been there and back in thirty minutes if we'd followed Geordie's suggestion and taken the campervan.' She resumes packing.

'It's not just yesterday, though, is it? We lurch from one catastrophe to another. Oh, yes, we may get six or so months of relative normality, but then, sure enough, he'll do something stupid again.'

'How long have you been married, now? Eight years?'

She nods. 'Aye. Eight years of ups and downs.'

'I've known him for twenty-two years.'

'I know that. Does it get any easier?'

I laugh. 'It takes a while, but yes, it does. I remember during our second world tour; I woke up one morning in a hotel room. I must have been about twenty. I had a black-eye and bloodied knuckles. I can't recall exactly what happened. We'd either been to a nightclub or a curry house and got in a fight. It wasn't the first time. I've never witnessed Geordie start a fight… ever. But he will put his body on the line when he sees injustice or bullying. It had been an arduous week. Geordie was forever squabbling with Flaky and Chas. We'd been busted for drugs and then arrested again for smashing up a hotel room, which may I add, we weren't the culprits. It was the support band. I'd tried everything I could to change him. I gave him books to read that I thought would broaden his mind. I suggested he take up meditation. I tried to get him to cut down on the booze and focus on the music. Nothing worked.'

'He sounded like a nightmare,' Jackie murmurs.

'He was. I had a decision to make; kick him out of the band or keep him in. That's when I realised, it wasn't Geordie that had to change… it was me. So that's what I did. I realised that life was never going to be easy with him, but then again, life would never be dull.'

She sighs. 'You're not wrong there.'

235

'If you strip away the bullshit, bluster, and idiotic behaviour he's a *good* man who tries his best but sometimes gets it wrong,' I say. 'When I was lowering him down over the cliff yesterday, do you know what he said?'

She picks up a suitcase and throws it into the boot. 'Of course, I don't,' she replies sullenly.

'He said, watch out for Jackie and the kids… financially. He realised there was a good chance he could die. But he was determined to save Wallace. And yet… his last worry was about you and the boys not about himself.'

She stares at the ground. 'Christ,' she murmurs.

'He's a lifeforce, albeit uncoordinated, but a lifeforce, nevertheless.'

'Oh, aye, he's that all right. But a lifeforce can be draining when it sucks everything out of you,' she says. I stub my ciggy out and rub her shoulder.

'True. But as my Grandma used to say, "we're a long time dead. Live life on the edge." Wise words.'

'What did your Grandma do for a living?'

'She was a cleaner at the local gas plant.' Jackie cracks a smile but restrains herself from laughing. 'Despite his faults, of which there are many, he has a heart as big as a balloon. He means well.'

She gazes at me, glassy-eyed. 'I suppose he does. I cannae deny that.'

'Daddy, daddy!' Mary calls out as she comes running up. 'Can we come camping again? This is the bestest holiday I've ever had. Can we stay another day?'

'We'll come camping again but we can't stay another day. Sorry sweet pea.'

'But why?' she pouts. 'You don't work.'

I chuckle. 'Actually, I do. I make music.'

'That's not proper work, though, is it?'

'Let's call it different work. It pays for camping holidays, ice creams, and funfairs. Anyway, guess who will be waiting for us to get home?'

'Who?' she asks as she hands me her kite to dismantle.

'Our poor old doggy, Caesar.'

'Oh, yes!' she screams. 'Can we get him today?'

'Yes... but only if we get back in time. That's why we need to set off now. The kennels close at five.' As I take Mary's hand and head to the campervan, Jackie calls out.

'Will, when you said it was you who had to change, not Geordie, what exactly did you mean?'

'I meant, I had to stop trying to make him into something I wanted him to be. I had to accept him... warts and all.'

'Thanks, Will... I think I finally get it.'

I smile and shrug. 'As I said, it takes a while.'

Thank You For Reading

I hope you enjoyed this book in the Shooting Star series. If you want to read the next instalment, there's an extract below of the boys' new adventure titled, **"I Will Survive"**. This involves our hapless gang participating in a "Celebrity Survivor" challenge on a desert island in the South Pacific. It is on pre-order here–The Shooting Star Series–I Will Survive.

If you've missed any of the books in the series, there's a reading order below, although, each book can be read as a standalone.

If you wish to keep up to date with my book news, there are a few simple ways to be notified.

You can subscribe to my entertaining, monthly "Discombobulated" newsletter. This not only keeps you abreast of new releases, but I sometimes have a free book to giveaway or heavy discounts throughout the year. It's also a good laugh–there's no hard sell–I promise. You can sign up by following the link below which will take you to my website.

I would like to subscribe to your newsletter.

Alternatively, you can go to the following sites and click on the "Follow" button, which should give you new release alerts.

BookBub

Amazon

Facebook

For paperback readers, the links above won't work no matter how many times you tap your finger on them. Below is a manual link to my newsletter to type into your browser.

https://www.subscribepage.com/author_simon_northouse_home

All **reviews** are appreciated.

If you would like to contact me personally, here's my email address.

simon@simonnorthouse.com–I always enjoy a chat and will reply.

THE SHOOTING STAR SERIES

Book 1: Arc Of A Shooting Star

Book 2: Catch A shooting Star

Book 3: Fall Of A Shooting Star

Book 4: What's It All About... Geordie

Book 5: Nuts At Christmas (Novella)

Book 6: Eggs Unscrambled

Book 7: I Will Survive

Book 8: Bells At New Year - Release Date November 2021

I Will Survive - Chapter 1: Stranded

I pull a knife from my belt, sit down on a sun-bleached log and whittle. I stare out at Flaky, who is frolicking in the sea about twenty metres away.

'Daft bastard,' I murmur to myself. Spreadeagled on the white sand in front of me is Geordie. The numbnut is sunbathing. His Scottish, alabaster skin is already turning a pink hue under the blazing Sun. The canopy from a palm tree protects me from the celestial fireball but not the humidity, which is strength sapping. There's a rustle of leaves and the snapping of twigs behind me. I glance over my shoulder to witness Robbo emerging from the thick jungle. He pulls the fly up on his shorts as he ambles towards me.

'Hey, Will, I'm not sure how much more of this I can take,' he whines, bitterly. 'No weed, no pixie dust, no alcohol, not even any smokes. I can't last much longer.' I glance at my watch.

'We've only been here four hours,' I reply wearily.

'Exactly! What am I going to be like after four weeks!' he exclaims.

'Fit, detoxed, your body once again a temple of purity. I think they were your words when this hairbrained idea was first raised. Be careful what you wish for.' Flaky emerges from the sea and runs back to us like an eager teenager. He grabs a towel off the sand and vigorously rubs himself down.

'Oh, wow! Isn't this magnificent? Isn't it wonderful?'

'No,' I say.

'The calm, the serenity. Man, and nature living in harmony.' Geordie rolls onto his front and lets out a rasping fart as he does so.

'There goes the serenity,' Robbo comments.

'And the harmony,' I add. Flaky throws Geordie a prudish glance but says nothing. He stops drying himself and stares at me.

'What are you doing?' he asks.

'What does it look like I'm doing… I'm whittling.'

'I can see that, but what are you whittling?'

'A stick.'

'I can see it's a bloody stick! But what is the ultimate purpose?' he shouts, getting annoyed.

'A spear to kill things with,' I answer, glumly.

'Hmm, well, I won't be killing any of God's creatures. There's an abundance of vegetation, fruit, nuts, and fresh water on this island to make the eating of meat totally unnecessary.' I scrape a few more pieces of wood from the tip of the spear and touch the point with my finger.

'Yep, that should do it,' I say. I get to my feet, do a quick run up and release the missile with a half-hearted throw. The stick wobbles as it flies through the air before landing horizontally about fifteen metres down the beach. 'Hmm, it needs more weight on the tip. It could also do with some fletching, give it more stability,' I add thoughtfully.

'Fletching?' Robbo queries. 'Isn't that a perverse sexual practice?'

'That's felching, you moron,' I reply. 'Fletching is the craft of attaching feathers to the end, like an arrow.' I turn and glare at Flaky. 'So, you reckon you're going to last four weeks on this island by scrimmaging around in the jungle trying to find a turnip or two?' Flaky laughs, in a pompous sort of way, an annoying trait of his.

'I've done my research, Will. God's larder is bursting at the seams. There's breadfruit, ruka, seaweed, chillies, yams, sweet potatoes, bananas, oranges, coconuts, custard apples, mangoes—the list goes on and on.'

'A bit like you,' Geordie mumbles.

'I'll bet you that within a week you'll be ripping flesh from a bone with your bare teeth,' I barter. Flaky hangs his towel over a branch of a tree and sniggers.

'William, my good friend, I was a vegan for over twenty years, a vegetarian for a year and a pescatarian for over six months. Why would you think I would suddenly turn into a raging carnivore in the space of a week?' I sit back down on the log and let out a deep sigh.

'Because you lot don't know what you've got us into,' I begin.

'I do,' Robbo curses.

'It may be easy to be a pescatarian at home, when you can nip down to the supermarket and get your broccolini, a bunch of asparagus tips and a fillet of smoked salmon—not so here. In a week's time you will be ravenous and fatigued from hunger. Your gut will ache with emptiness and you, my good friend, will succumb.' Flaky smiles benevolently at me.

'My resolve is tempered in the cauldron of righteousness. I will survive.'

'Christ, Flaky, you sound like Billy Graham,' Geordie moans as he sits upright, squinting at us. The distant sound of engines distracts me as I peer down the beach. Heading towards us is a red quad bike followed by a yellow, two-man, all-terrain-vehicle with roll bars and cargo netting.

'Eh up,' I begin, 'looks like our glorious leader is heading our way.' The others turn and stare at the rapidly approaching vehicles.

'I've never been able to take to Gerrard,' Robbo drawls.

'No, me neither,' Geordie agrees. 'He's a pompous prig. Never trust a man that wears a cravat.'

'You two are so judgemental,' Flaky bristles. 'Just because he's got a posh accent, is well-educated, and successful, you have it in for him. You're both inverted snobs.'

'It's nowt to do with that,' Robbo replies. 'I don't care what background or upbringing anyone's had. I take each man, or woman, on their own merits and Gerrard is a twat of the highest order.' The vehicles stop about ten feet away and the occupants alight.

'Christ, what *is* he wearing?' Geordie murmurs as he slowly shakes his head. Gerrard is sporting a pale grey safari suit with a pink cravat adorned around his neck. In his left hand he holds a black walking stick with an ornate ferrule attached on the top. He prowls towards us in a flamboyant, over-energetic manner, as if trying to prove he's younger than his sixty years.

'He's forgot his monocle,' Robbo chuckles.

'Ah, chaps!' Gerrard calls out. 'Sorry for the delay. I've had word the last of the contestants are about to be choppered in within the next thirty minutes. We can't begin until everyone is safely on the island, otherwise it could be deemed you had an unfair advantage.' The other two guys, who for some bizarre reason are dressed like Australian lifeguards, in red and yellow shorts and shirts, grab a large trunk from the back of the ATV and follow Gerard.

'What's in the box?' Flaky asks, with a welcoming smile.

'Basic provisions,' Gerrard says. The two guys drop the box in front of us as Gerrard squats, releases a clasp on the box, and throws the lid open in dramatic fashion. He lists the contents. 'Sixty feet of climbing rope, a ball of string, a small shovel, and a first-aid kit. Four mess kits containing a metal plate, cup, knife and fork and small kettle. A canteen, a hunting knife with steel and machetes.'

'That's handy,' I say, 'because if we were stranded on a desert island in the middle of the South Pacific, I'm not sure we'd stumble across a metal trunk containing all this clobber.' Gerrard eyes me suspiciously as he rises and stretches his back.

'Aye, very fortuitous,' Geordie scoffs as he bends down and picks up a machete and runs his thumb along the edge of the blade.

'Let me make it clear,' begins Gerrard, 'that foremost this is a TV program. It is entertainment. If we didn't provide you with some basic equipment, I'm not sure any of you would survive more than a couple of days, let alone four weeks. You still must forage for your own food and water and make your own shelter. Talking of which, Travis,' he says as he fixes his attention on one of the young muscular guys with a shock of sun-bleached blonde hair.

'Yes, Gerrard?' Travis replies in a slightly effeminate tone.

'Could you show the Shooting Tsars to their camp and explain the set up to them?'

'Of course, Gerrard. Delighted to,' he says, fluttering his eyelashes. Geordie's eyes furtively swivel towards me then Robbo.

'Once the last team arrives, we'll give them an hour to settle in, then we'll hold a meet and greet at HQ,' Gerrard explains as he turns to leave. As quick as a flash, Geordie throws his forearm around Gerrard's neck and holds the machete to his throat.

'One false move and you're a dead man,' Geordie whispers in his ear. Gerrard's body stiffens as his two helpers stand frozen to the spot with a look of horror on their faces. Geordie winks at me.

'What are you, you, do… doing?' Gerrard stammers.

'I'm hungry and there's plenty of meat on you. Remember the show's motto? Survival at any cost. There's nothing in the rules about cannibalism.' Geordie swiftly pulls the machete across Gerrard's neck. He lets out a high-pitched scream as his hands clutch at his throat. Geordie laughs like a drain as Gerrard inspects his hands, expecting to see blood.

'You bloody idiot!' Flaky yells. 'What did you do that for?'

'Oh, calm down, pencil dick, it was only a joke! I used the back of the blade. I thought it would lighten the mood.' Gerrard's expression doesn't convince me he got the joke. I think he may have soiled himself.

'I don't appreciate practical jokes like that,' he says, scowling at the oaf.

'Relax, man. No harm done.' Gerrard turns and marches back to the ATV.

'Travis, I'll see you over at the Celebrity Chefs camp once you've finished with this bunch.'

'Very good, Gerrard,' Travis says. 'Okay boys, if two of you would like to grab your box, no pun intended, and follow me. I'll lead you to your living quarters for at least the next four weeks.'

*****

Our camp is about a ten-minute walk inland, away from the beach through dense brush and forest. There is a discernible track, but it's overgrown and will need clearing if it's to be our primary route, to and from the beach.

We arrive at a clearing, about fifteen metres in diameter. The dense canopy of the jungle provides welcome relief from the heat of the Sun. Four hammocks are already set up close to each other, strung between giant palm trees.

'The biggest danger on this island,' Travis begins, 'isn't from insects, snakes or wild boars, it's from falling coconuts. If one hits you on the head, then it's goodnight Vienna. We've made sure the hammocks are attached to trees that don't have any nuts on them, so at least you'll be able to sleep easy on a night.'

'How very thoughtful of you,' Geordie says. 'What number do I need to dial for Room Service?' he sneers as he wanders off to inspect the camp. I pull a handkerchief from my pocket and wipe the sweat from my brow.

'I've never slept in a hammock before,' Flaky states as he tries to climb into one. After a few failed attempts, he manages it. 'Ooh, I quite like this. The distant sound of the ocean, the chatter of birds, the chirrup of insects—it's all very relaxing and peaceful. I think I'm going to be thrilled here.' *Bloody buffoon! He's still living in a fantasy world of the Swiss Family Robinson.* Geordie walks up to Flaky and lifts one edge of the hammock, sending Flaky sprawling to the ground.

'You great big lumbering neanderthal!' Flaky yells. 'What the hell did you do that for?'

'This is my hammock,' Geordie growls. 'It's longer than all the rest.' Travis leans into me and whispers.

'Is Geordie... you now... mentally stable?' He carries a worried frown on his face. I stare back at him.

'It depends on your definition of stable. His behaviour at the moment is completely normal. However, when the shit hits the fan and things don't go his way, he has been known to become slightly erratic.' Travis tries to smile, but it looks more like a grimace. He points up at one of the palm trees.

'There's the camera mounted about ten feet up,' he says. 'When it's live, you'll see a red led light flashing. On the tree next to it is a loudspeaker. Whenever it's time for a new challenge or meeting, Gloria Gaynor's "I Will Survive" will play. That's your prompt to make your way to the games area near HQ. That was my idea,' he adds, looking pleased with himself. 'We can also speak to you directly in case of emergencies,' he adds.

'What sort of emergencies?'

'Oh, you know, bushfire, cyclone warning, stingers.'

'Stingers?'

'Yes. Poisonous jellyfish.'

'Great. What about sharks?'

'This is a coral island, so it's mainly reef sharks. They're not dangerous... usually. Right, I better get going. I'll see you at the meet and greet later. Remember, when you hear Gloria sing, that's your cue to make your way to HQ. Chin chin! Oh, and watch out for the leeches,' he calls out as he heads back through the dense bush. I watch him leave as a sense of foreboding swamps me. I gaze over at Flaky, Robbo and Geordie, who are already bickering about where the campfire should be located.

Poisonous jellyfish, sharks which may or may not be dangerous, wild boars, killer coconuts, snakes, stinging insects, leeches and three first-class morons to contend with, not to mention Gloria Gaynor—what did I do to deserve this?

Place Your Pre-Order Here From Amazon–I Will Survive

About the Author

Simon Northouse is the author of:

The Shooting Star series

The Soul Love series

The School Days series

Let's Get Discombobulated Newsletters series

Printed in Great Britain
by Amazon